Book Two

EPIC ZERO 2

Tales of a Pathetic Power Failure

By

R.L. Ullman

But That's Another Story... Press

Published by But That's Another Story… Press
Ridgefield, CT

Printed in the United States of America.

First Printing, 2016.

All character images created with heromachine.com.

ISBN: 978-0-9964921-5-7
Library of Congress Control Number: 2016901256

For Lynn,
my Wonder Woman

BOOKS BY R.L. ULLMAN

EPIC ZERO SERIES

PRAISE FOR EPIC ZERO
Readers' Favorite Gold Medal Award Winner

"What a fun read! I knew this was a great children's/young adult book when my 11-year-old kept trying to read it over my shoulder. This is a delightful read for children and tweens, even for children who don't always enjoy reading. I loved the main character, I loved the message, I loved the illustrations; I just plain loved this book." **Rating: 5.0 stars by Tracy A. Fischer for Readers' Favorite.**

"An awesome and inspirational coming of age story filled with superheroes, arch villains and lots of action. Most highly recommended." **Rating: 5.0 stars by Jack Magnus for Readers' Favorite.**

"With Epic Zero, Ullman reminds me of why I used to love superheroes. If the other books are anything like this one, then the whole series will be great." **Rating 5.0 stars by Jessyca Garcia for Readers' Favorite.**

"As if a good read wasn't enough. Ullman goes that extra mile by adding illustrations and statistics, as well as a Meta glossary of terms and superpowers. These added features will appeal to those boys and girls who enjoy the science in science fiction." **Rating 5.0 stars by Francine Zane for Readers' Favorite.**

GET MORE EPIC FREE!

Don't miss any of the action! Get a FREE copy of Epic Zero 1.5: Tales of a Serious Superhero Screw Up.

Get your FREE book exclusively from the author's website: rlullman.com.

TABLE OF CONTENTS

ONE

I MUST BE THE LAMEST SUPERHERO EVER

Truthfully, I should've been blasted to smithereens by now. But somehow, I'm still standing

I slide across the hood of a parked car, wrap my cape around my derriere, and duck beneath the window. I desperately need a few seconds to catch my breath. Here I am, supposedly the most powerful superhero in the universe, about to eat it big time.

I hear crunching in the distance. I stay as still as a mouse in a snake pit. The thought, "please fall into a manhole," auto loops in my brain.

But no such luck.

The crunching gets louder and louder, closer and

closer, until suddenly, it stops.

I hold my breath, the silence drags on for an eternity.

Then, there's a whirring noise.

I bolt from the car just as I hear the FOOP of a missile launcher. The vehicle blows sky-high, the force of it propels me into the air, over a spiked fence, and headfirst onto a schoolyard blacktop. I tuck my head into my knees and roll it out, but when I pop up my left shoulder is on fire with pain. It feels dislocated.

But hey, it's not all bad news. Fortunately, it's the middle of the night, so there aren't any kids around. That means, the only life at stake is my own. And, at least for the moment, it saves me from more embarrassment.

Which is basically how my family sees me.

You see, I live in a family of superheroes—not just any yahoos in tights and capes—but members of the Freedom Force, the greatest team of Metas on the planet. A "Meta" is short for Meta-being—which is basically a person, animal, or vegetable (yeah, I know you've probably heard this before) with powers and abilities far beyond the scope of ordinary beings. There are nine Meta types, including: Energy Manipulation, Flight, Magic, Meta-Morphing, Psychic, Super-Intelligence, Super-Speed, Super-Strength, and the newest one—Meta Manipulation.

Each power type can be further broken down into power levels. A Meta 1 has limited power, a Meta 2 has considerable power, and a Meta 3 has extreme power. If you don't have any powers at all, then you're known as a Meta 0—or a "Zero" for short—which basically means you're powerless.

That used to be me, but not anymore.

Although sometimes I'm not so sure.

I'm a Meta Manipulator with the ability to negate the powers of others. Basically my powers can turn any Meta 1, 2, or 3—into a 0. Other than Meta-Taker, the baddest of all bad guys who croaked in the battle at Lockdown, I'm the only Meta Manipulator around.

And, as I demonstrated when I took control of the Orb of Oblivion—a cosmic entity of ridiculous power— and saved the world from the Skelton—a demented race of alien shapeshifters, I'm pretty powerful myself. The latest tests have me down as a Meta 3.

On the surface, everything seems hunky-dory. I've got superpowers, I'm on the Freedom Force, I get to call myself Epic Zero, wear long johns and fight bad guys. I'm living the dream!

So, what's the problem? Well, that's the funny thing.

My powers *are* my problem.

Let me give you an example. Two weeks ago, the Meta Monitor picked up a break-in at ArmaTech, a government contracted weapons manufacturer. So, we loaded into the Freedom Flyer III and made it to the scene, only to find the Destruction Crew, a band of Meta 2 supervillains, shaking down the joint.

It had been a while since I went on a mission, so I

thought I'd remind everybody of what I can do.

As soon as the Freedom Flyer skidded to a stop, I jumped into action. I figured if I could use my abilities to negate the Destruction Crew's powers, the fight would be over before it started. Yep, that was the plan.

You should have seen how surprised those goons were when I marched out in front of them. Hey, I get it. I'm just a short, skinny 12-year-old kid. But Mom always says to never judge a book by its cover.

So, after they stopped laughing, I went to work. I concentrated like my life depended on it, and pushed my Meta Manipulation energy all over them. But they just shrugged me off. That is, until they tried to use their powers.

You should have seen their faces when nothing happened! It was awesome! I thought this superhero thing was a cakewalk.

But then, Dad, who goes by the handle Captain Justice, couldn't use his Super-Strength.

And Mom, also known as Ms. Understood, couldn't use her Psychic abilities.

And it was the same story for the rest of the Freedom Force: including my sister Grace, who goes by Glory Girl, and TechnocRat, Master Mime, Blue Bolt and Makeshift.

I guess you could say my powers worked *too* well!

Once the Destruction Crew realized we were *all* powerless, well, that's when things got ugly.

Real ugly.

"Grab the kid!" one of the villains yelled.

They rushed me, took me hostage, and nearly escaped with me in our own Freedom Flyer! If it wasn't for the street fighting skills of Shadow Hawk, the only one of us who didn't have Meta powers to begin with, I'd probably be six feet under right now.

I admit that was pretty bad.

But then, it got worse.

"Sorry, Elliott," Dad said. "You're suspended."

"Suspended?" I said. "You mean, like, no longer on the team?"

"Yes," Dad said. "Exactly like that."

Dad basically told me I'm on the bench until I can better control my powers.

Are! You! Freaking! Kidding! Me!

So now I'm off the team. At least, until I can prove I deserve to be back in the starting rotation.

Which is why I find myself in my current predicament.

The guy hunting me down is named Buzzkill. He's a cyborg—part human, part robot with Meta 2 Super-Strength and a generally nasty attitude. Neutralizing his Meta powers was easy enough. But now I'm a moving target for the ridiculous array of weapons he can conjure up from the mechanical-side of his body.

Unfortunately, my Meta power has no effect on standard criminal tools-of-the-trade; including knives, throwing stars, guns, lasers, spitballs and, present case in point, heat-seeking missiles.

So, I'm in a wee bit of trouble.

I hustle off the school grounds and hang a right down the first alleyway I see. How am I going to deal with this guy before he obliterates me? I peer over my shoulder, but Buzzkill's nowhere in sight.

That's when I trip over a spilled garbage can and smash face-first into a brick wall.

Everything goes dark for a moment before I realize I'm flat on my back on a pile of trash bags. My nose is throbbing and there's a warm, wet drizzle on my upper lip. Instinctively, I wipe it. Yep, it's blood.

Marvelous.

I've literally run into a dead-end. What superhero does that?

I try to stand up, but my body has other ideas. I'm still shaking out the cobwebs when I sense the area around me darkening. I look up, only to find Buzzkill standing over me, blocking out the moonlight.

"Hello, possum," he says with his deep, synthesized voice. His red, mechanical eye flickers in its socket like a metal-detector that's hit the jackpot.

"Can we talk about this?" I ask.

Buzzkill extends his left arm. His robotic fingers retract into his wrist socket, only to be replaced with a giant spinning buzz saw. "Certainly, Epic Zero" he says. "Shall we dissect your situation piece by piece?"

Well, this sucks.

Buzzkill amps up his buzz saw, and then swings at me.

I barely roll out of the way as he slices through a stack of bricks like a hot knife through butter. That was lucky! But he's not finished. Buzzkill wheels around for another shot. I spring to my feet, searching for a way out, but he's blocking the only exit!

I back up against the wall like a trapped animal. My shoulder is still throbbing, and my nose is spewing blood like a faucet.

The human-half of Buzzkill's face lights up in a menacing smile. "Game over, Zero," he says, revving his buzz saw to full throttle.

My heart is pounding. All I can think is *why*? *Why* can't I have super-strength like Dad, and break this guy in two? *Why* can't I use telepathy like Mom, and knock him to his knees? *Why* can't I fly out of here like Grace? *Why* am I so ... lame?

Suddenly, Buzzkill steps forward and pins me against the wall by my neck!

He's gripping so tight I can't breathe! I want to end this, but I can't say the words ...

His buzz saw is rotating so fast it's nearly invisible. Then, Buzzkill lurches back to deliver the deathblow.

I close my eyes.

This is gonna be messy.

"Drop the pizza cutter, Buzzkill!" comes a familiar

voice. "The kid's all mine!"

I open my eyes to find a woman's dark, gloved hand wrapped around Buzzkill's mechanical wrist. And then, I watch Mom sock the villain square across the jaw, sending him flying.

"GISMO, end program!" Mom shouts, rubbing her knuckles.

"Training module ended, Ms. Understood," comes GISMO's warm, mechanical voice.

Instantly, Buzzkill and the alleyway disappear, leaving Mom and me all alone in the stark white confines of the Combat Room.

Based on Mom's expression, I suddenly wish Buzzkill finished the job.

"Elliott Harkness!" Mom lays into me, "What in the world are you doing here? You're supposed to be sleeping."

I try to avoid Mom's penetrating glare, but even if I avert that, I can't escape her superhero insignia of a giant eye which is staring me down, compelling me to tell the truth—or maybe it's just a mom power. Unfortunately, I don't have a good get-out-of- jail-free card.

"I'm sorry," I say, sheepishly. "I'm just trying to get some extra practice."

"I see," Mom says. "Well, next time set GISMO on an easier training module. If I hadn't tracked you down, who knows what could have happened down here."

GISMO is short for Global Intelligence Simulation

Model Operator. GISMO runs the Combat Room where the Freedom Force hones their powers. The Combat Room can create any situation imaginable, including my near-death experience with Buzzkill.

"Good thinking, Mom," I say, sarcastically. "Because you know real villains will let me off the hook if I just ask them to go easy on me. If I can't defeat them in a crummy training module, then what chance do I have on a real mission? I'll never be back on the team."

"Elliott," Mom says, putting her hand on my shoulder. "You've got to give yourself time to develop. You'll get there."

"Yeah," I say, "like when I'm eighty."

"Oh, Elliott," she sighs.

Just then, there's a loud crackle overhead. "Freedom Force to the Mission Room," comes TechnocRat's high-pitched voice over the intercom system. "Freedom Force to the Mission Room."

Mom and I hightail it out of the Combat Room, and hit the East Wing stairwell. Oh, I should probably mention that we live in a satellite headquarters in outer space called the Waystation. The views of Earth are amazing, but it can get pretty lonely when you're left up here all by yourself.

Which I'm guessing is exactly what's about to happen to me.

We make it up to the Mission Room to find all of the heroes gathered: Dad, TechnocRat, Blue Bolt, Master

Mime, Shadow Hawk, Makeshift, and my 14-year-old sister, Grace.

"Nice of you to finally join us," she says sourly, her arms folded across her chest.

"Sorry, we had an old tin can to dispose of," Mom says, winking at me. "What's going on?"

TechnocRat scampers onto the keypad and starts typing rapidly with his pink paws and tail. "Moments ago, we received a distress signal. A rather unusual distress signal. Take a look."

The giant screen powers on, and there's an image of a muscular, mustached man wearing a red mask and bodysuit with an insignia of a black atom on his chest. I know him immediately from his Meta profile. It's the Atomic Rage.

"Freedom Force," he says, desperately. "You have to help us!"

The terror in his voice sets the hairs on my neck on end. The Atomic Rage is a major supervillain—a Meta 3 Energy Manipulator that can fire bolts of explosive, atomic energy. He's no chump change. So, why's he so freaked out?

"He's coming for us!" the Atomic Rage continues, his eyes bulging wide. "He's coming for us all! Help us! Please! Help—"

And then, the video cuts out.

"Well that was awkward," Grace says.

"What's that all about?" Blue Bolt asks, downing

four power bars in a millisecond. "Besides, isn't he part of the Ominous Eight. Was he referring to them?"

TechnocRat's nose starts twitching. "Unfortunately, we're not sure. That's all of the transmission we received. The Meta Monitor pinpointed the location of the last power signature for the Atomic Rage. I also have readings for the rest of the Ominous Eight. I think we should investigate."

"Hold on," Grace says, "You want *us* to help those villains? What do we care if they eat each other? I mean, isn't that a good thing?"

"We're heroes," Dad says, "We're sworn to help all of those in need. Whether they're villains or not."

I glance over at Makeshift who smiles back.

"What if it's a trap?" Shadow Hawk asks.

"The thought crossed my mind as well," Dad says. "But I don't think the Atomic Rage is that good an actor. Nevertheless, whether it's a trap or if there really *is* someone powerful enough to take down the Atomic Rage and the Ominous Eight, we'd better bring the whole team."

"Great idea, Dad," I declare, "I call shotgun!"

Dad puts his hand on my shoulder. Here it comes.

"Sorry, Elliott," he says. "You're still suspended."

Of course I am.

"Freedom Force," Dad says. "It's Fight Time!"

The heroes pour out of the room.

Mom lingers behind. "And Elliott, no—"

"—Combat Room," I finish. "Yeah, I got it."

I watch her leave, and then feel a soft nuzzle against my hand. Dog-Gone, our German Shepherd who can turn invisible, materializes beside me.

"Well, at least you didn't abandon me," I say, petting his head. "I guess we should grab a snack and go to bed. C'mon, let's see what's in the Galley."

Dog-Gone licks his lips.

We're halfway there when—

"Alert! Alert! Alert!" the Meta Monitor blares. "Meta 3 disturbance. Repeat: Meta 3 disturbance. Identity unknown. Alert! Alert! Alert! Meta 3 disturbance. Identity unknown."

Dog-Gone and I hustle to the Meta Monitor room.

The Meta Monitor is our computer system that detects Meta powers. The Meta Monitor can read disturbances in the Earth's molecular structure. Like fingerprints, each and every super power leaves a distinct Meta signature. The Meta Monitor reads this signature and matches it with its database of Metas to determine who, or what, may have caused it.

I hop into the leather command chair, punch a few codes into the keyboard, and up pops an image of an abandoned warehouse. There's a red call-out that reads: *Identity Unknown.*

Whoever's causing the Meta Monitor to go bonkers must be in there.

Unfortunately, the Freedom Force is off saving the

Ominous Eight. Somebody ought to check it out. But, there's nobody around but us.

I look down at Dog-Gone, who answers back with a low growl.

Scratch that.

It seems there's nobody around …

But me.

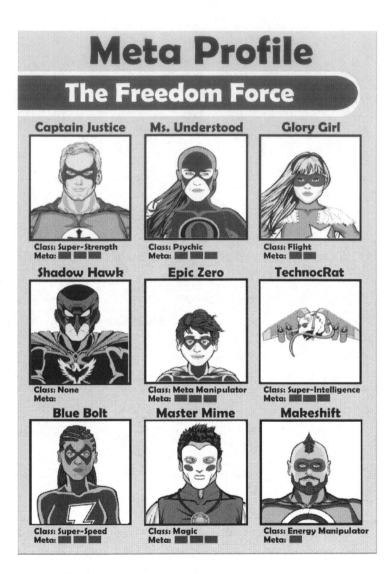

TWO

I SEE WHY CURIOSITY KILLED THE CAT

I know I shouldn't be doing this.

But, I'm betting that hauling in a real villain will do more to convince my parents to put me back on the team than completing some training module. Of course, this could all be for naught if I get toasted.

So, here's to hoping that doesn't happen.

I give Dog-Gone the slip by baiting him with doggie treats and locking him in the Galley. Boy, is he upset. I'm five levels down in the Hanger, and I can still hear him howling. I feel terrible, but thankfully dogs can't talk, so I know he won't be snitching on me anytime soon.

I hop into one of our brand-spanking new Freedom

Ferries and jet to Earth. The Freedom Ferry is TechnocRat's latest invention. It's basically a slimmed down version of the Freedom Flyer, designed to transport up to three people from the Waystation to Earth and back again. After having two Freedom Flyers demolished in less than a year and building a third one, TechnocRat says he won't have to attend as many anger management classes when we inevitably wreck one of the Ferries.

But getting blown out of the sky isn't on the agenda.

I'm on a stealth mission.

It's early morning when I touch down, landing perfectly in a clearing in the middle of a forest, hundreds of yards from my destination. Admittedly, getting there is going to be a haul, but I don't want the noise of my rocket-powered shuttle giving me away.

I carefully pick my way through the underbrush, my costume catching on so many thorns I look like I've gone twelve rounds with a pack of angry porcupines. After a while, my skin starts itching all over, giving me the horrifying thought that I may be wading through miles of poison ivy.

Freaking fabulous.

Then, through a small opening in the trees, I spot the warehouse.

It's a huge building that's clearly seen better days. Swaths of beige siding cling loosely to the exterior, boarded windows line the building, and the lawn clearly hasn't been mowed in years. The only sign of life comes from a chimney on the far side of the roof that's pumping out black smoke.

Which means someone's inside.

I don't see any security cameras or obvious booby traps, so I make a mad dash for the back door. When I get there, I press snugly against the rotting wall. The only sound I hear is my own beating heart—and goodness, isn't that deafeningly loud for a so-called superhero?

Now, I just need to get inside—undetected.

I grab the door handle, roll my wrist, and pull. The door swings open with a screech so loud you'd think I let loose a colony of bats.

So much for the element of surprise.

Now I know why Shadow Hawk carries WD-40 in his utility belt.

I decide to lay low, just in case I've given myself away. I wait a good five minutes, trying to breathe as little as humanly possible. Since no one came to kill me, I consider the coast to be clear. I count to three, and slip inside.

It's dark—pitch dark.

I reach into my belt, and pull out my flashlight, thankful I had the foresight to rummage through the Freedom Ferry's glove compartment before leaving the ship behind. I thought it might come in handy—Master Mime's extra ketchup packets, not so much.

I turn on the flashlight, and shine it around.

The inside of the warehouse is cavernous. Wooden,

brown crates are stacked stories high on metal fixtures. There's a catwalk bolted to the ceiling, traversing the fixtures, and providing a bird's-eye view of the facility. Dust-covered forklifts are scattered all about, seemingly untouched for years.

There's a bunch of doors along the perimeter, all of them closed. Nothing seems particularly unusual, until my flashlight hits the last door on the right.

It's cracked open.

Bingo!

I slowly make my way over, careful not to knock over a crate, fall into a vat, or step onto some imaginary clown's horn my mind keeps placing in front of my feet. When I finally reach the door, I crane my neck, listening intently. All I hear is a low humming noise.

At this point, I have two options—enter the dark, scary room, or go home and face a really ticked off German Shepherd.

I came all this way, so logically I should probably see it through. So, why isn't my body moving?

Truthfully, I have no idea who, or what, is behind this door. It could be mothballs and packing tape, or it could be the freakiest Meta villain in the history of caped crusading. Of course, if I were a real superhero I'd just step inside and deal with whatever came my way, but I'm not on the Freedom Force anymore, am I? So, I guess there's no obligation to go any further.

Then, I think about what Dad would do.

And then I wonder why I had to think about that.

Well, here goes nothing.

I take a deep breath, and enter the room.

A musty smell attacks my nostrils. I notice the room is windowless, which means it's somehow even darker than the main part of the warehouse. It's freezing in here, and my body starts shaking like a leaf. The temperature must be thirty degrees colder than the rest of the building. What gives?

I scan the interior with my flashlight. More crates. A stack of brown boxes. An empty storage rack. A broken conveyer belt. A mustached face. A pile of coffee cups. A ... a ...

I scream.

Flight mode kicks in, and I bolt from the room, my blood pumping in my ears. I've got to get out of here! I've got to get back to the Waystation! I've got to ... to ...

Wait a second!

I look behind me, and realize I'm not being chased. Did I really see what I thought I saw? Or, is my mind playing tricks on me?

I take a deep breath and re-enter the room, aiming my flashlight in the direction of the disturbing face. The light catches it full on. Yep, it's real—a pale, square-jawed face of a mustached, masked man. His eyes are closed, and he's wearing a red mask. But there's more than a face.

I scan down to his chest, his atom insignia flickering

in the light.

It's the Atomic Rage!

I shine the flashlight all around. He's standing stock-still in some sort of a chamber. And he's not alone!

To his left are more chambers! Lots of them!

Fire Fiend ... Airess ... Die-Abolical ... Think Tank ... Back Breaker ... Frightmare ... Rundown ....

It's the Ominous Eight!

They're all here! Unconscious!

I step closer to the Atomic Rage's chamber, and touch the outside. It's smooth, and cold, and vibrating. That humming noise is coming from the chambers themselves! It's like the Ominous Eight are trapped in ... refrigerators?

I shine my light on the Atomic Rage's face again, and notice tiny icicles hanging from his eyelashes and moustache. Someone's put them on ice! They're trapped in some kind of frozen sleep—like suspended animation. It's like they're being preserved for something.

Then I remember the Atomic Rage's distress message. Someone was coming for him. Someone was coming for all of the Ominous Eight!

And I must be standing in their secret lair!

I quickly deduce that I'm way out of my league.

I've got to get the Freedom Force!

I charge out of the storage room, but before I reach the exit, I notice something out of the corner of my eye.

Another door is open.

One that was closed before.

And the light is on.

My brain tells me to bolt. To get out of here as fast as I can, jump in the Freedom Ferry, and wait patiently for reinforcements.

But curiosity is pulling me towards the door.

I turn off my flashlight and grip it tight. It may be the only weapon I have. I know what I'm doing is incredibly stupid, but I can't stop my feet from advancing.

I peer into the doorway.

There's a large man in black leaning over a gigantic furnace. I follow the thick pipes as they run up the wall, and out the ceiling. This must be where the smoke was coming from! The man nonchalantly tends the fire, placing logs inside to keep it going.

Even though his back is facing me, it's impossible not to notice his broad shoulders and massive muscles. My senses start tingling. It's time to start listening to my brain. I'm about to scram when—

He turns.

I'm frozen.

His face is way younger than his physique suggests— he looks like a teenager! His skin is pale, and his hair is light blond, bordering on white. There's something oddly familiar about him.

"Can I help you?" he asks, his face breaking into a disconcerting smile.

"Um, nope," I answer. "Just passing through. You

wouldn't happen to know the fastest way out of here, would you?"

"As a matter of fact I do," he says, his blue eyes erupting into smoldering embers of red. "Unfortunately, that exit is closed."

The door slams shut behind me.

How'd he do that?

Then, I see a wave of black atoms flashing around his fists.

I've got a bad feeling about this.

"You're a Meta," he says. "Show me what you've got."

How'd he know that? I don't know who this guy is, but he's dangerous, with a capital D.

So, I go with my first instinct, and throw my flashlight at his head. As soon as it leaves my hand it stops in mid-air. Then, he twists his wrist, and it comes flying back at double the speed. I duck as it crashes straight through the wall behind me.

"Come on," he says, "You can do better than that. I can *feel* it."

Feel it, huh? Oh, he'll feel it alright.

I concentrate, and blanket him with all of the negation energy I can muster.

Suddenly, the red embers crackling around his eyes go out, and the atoms encircling his fists disappear.

There, he's powerless.

"Yes," he says smiling, his head back, almost soaking

it in. "Well played. You *are* powerful. Maybe I'll add you to my collection. You're Epic Zero, right?"

That's freaky. How does he know my name?

"Who are you?" I ask. My mind flips through every Meta profile I've studied, but comes up empty.

"Oh, you don't know me," he says. "But I know you. And if what I've heard and read about you is true, what you did at Lockdown against those aliens was impressive."

He takes a step towards me. This guy is huge. Even without powers, he could rip me to shreds.

"Let me solve the mystery for you," he says. "My name is Siphon, and I'm going to make every Meta on the planet my slave."

"Um, okay," I say, backing towards the door. "And, why would you want to do that?"

"Let's just say I need them," he says.

Need them? For what? And then I remember the Ominous Eight in their chambers.

Siphon must have used Airess' energy manipulation powers to turn the flashlight back on me! And before that he used Think Tank's psychic powers to shut the door! And the atoms circling his fists must be from the Atomic Rage!

"Hang on," I say, "You said you're name is Siphon. Like, you siphon the powers of others?"

"That's right," he says. "And I can't believe my luck that *you* wandered through that door."

"And, why is that?" I ask, nervously.

"Because you're the one who took away the only family I've ever known," he says.

What? Now I'm really lost. What's he talking about?

Then, his eyes flare up again, the red energy swirling wildly around his face.

But ... that's impossible! I made him powerless!

Suddenly, I realize where I've seen energy like that before. It couldn't be!

"Y-you're ... ," I stammer.

"Now you're getting it," Siphon says. "I'm Meta-Taker's son. Only I'm more powerful."

"Meta-Taker had a son?" I blurt out.

"Hard to believe, huh?" Siphon asks. "But I'm not surprised you don't know about me. I've spent my entire life hidden away, just like he wanted. My father always said we were different than everyone else. We didn't look like other people, we didn't age like other people, we didn't fit in. We couldn't trust heroes or villains, it was the two of us against the world. And then, one day, he disappeared. Without a mother, I struggled to survive on my own. But I learned how to use my powers to get what I needed. I made it work."

His eyes look sad, like he'd never told his story to anyone before. I couldn't imagine growing up so isolated—without a family. I know they get on my nerves, but not having them around ...

"And when I heard he finally returned," Siphon

continues. "I couldn't believe it. I was so excited to get back together. But then ... you killed him. And I swore I wouldn't hide in the shadows anymore."

I watch as his neck veins pop out.

"Look, I'm really sorry. I had no idea. But I swear to you, I didn't do it. I didn't kill your dad. It was the Skelton. Those aliens at Lockdown—they killed your father."

"So now," he says, "I'm going to show all Metas what it's like to fight for survival. What it's like to beg— to grovel. Especially you."

"Was that the dinner bell I heard?" I turn for the door, when a giant demon materializes in front of me! I back up, before realizing it's an illusion—he's using Frightmare's magic! I grab the doorknob when it suddenly becomes hot to the touch! I pull my hand away. Now Fire Fiend's power!

I turn to face Siphon. He raises his fists, the atoms from Atomic Rage's power swirling around them faster and faster. He's gonna vaporize me!

"Listen!" I yell, waving my arms in front of my face. "I didn't do it! I don't care how evil you are, no kid should suffer like you did!"

Siphon hesitates for a moment, staring at me.

And then, his whole body is encapsulated in a strange orange energy.

"Hey!" he screams.

The energy surrounds him. Engulfs him.

He starts lifting off the ground.

"What are you doing?" he yells. "Put me down! Let me go!"

But I don't know what's happening to him. I'm not doing anything.

"Let! Me! G—"

And then he vanishes into thin air.

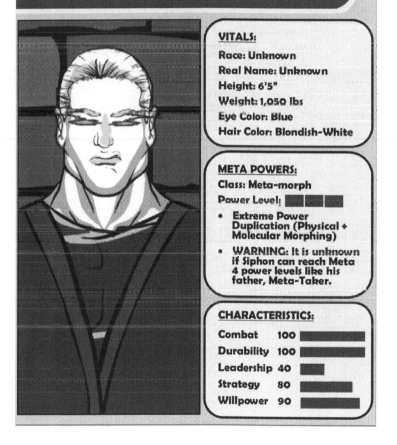

Meta Profile

Name: Siphon
Role: Villain   Status: Active

VITALS:

Race: Unknown
Real Name: Unknown
Height: 6'5"
Weight: 1,050 lbs
Eye Color: Blue
Hair Color: Blondish-White

META POWERS:

Class: Meta-morph
Power Level: ▮▮▮

- Extreme Power Duplication (Physical + Molecular Morphing)
- WARNING: It is unknown if Siphon can reach Meta 4 power levels like his father, Meta-Taker.

CHARACTERISTICS:

Combat	100	▬▬▬▬▬
Durability	100	▬▬▬▬▬
Leadership	40	▬▬
Strategy	80	▬▬▬▬
Willpower	90	▬▬▬▬

THREE

I DECIDE LIFE'S NOT FAIR

Sometimes there's no reward for doing the right thing.

I could have pretended the whole warehouse thing never happened. I could have returned the Freedom Ferry to its parking spot, refilled the tank with rocket fuel, and buffed it clean. I could have left the Ominous Eight in their freezers to become human popsicles. I could have said nothing about Siphon and his plans to rule over all Metas. I could have ignored the whole freaking thing.

But I couldn't do it.

I figured that if I want to *be* a superhero, then I need to *act* like a superhero. So, I called in the Freedom Force and told them everything.

And then my parents grounded me for a month.

Where's the justice in that?

Mom said I was impulsive, reckless, and obstinate.

Obstinate? Can you believe it?

I don't even know what that means!

Anyway, while I sat around fuming, the Freedom Force cleaned up the mess. Since the Ominous Eight were already on ice, TechnocRat simply transferred them in their cryo-chambers straight to Lockdown, the Meta-maximum security prison. TechnocRat said he'd build new cells for them once they got there.

So, I basically handed over eight Meta villains in one fell swoop. Did anyone say great job, Elliott? Nope. Did I get a pat on the back or a medal of honor? Nope.

Instead, I got punished.

And, to top it off, Dog-Gone is furious with me. Since we returned to the Waystation, he's basically given me the cold nose treatment. I tried making peace with a game of fetch, but he wasn't interested. I didn't know how serious it was until he walked away from a doggie treat. He'll come around eventually.

I hope.

So, everyone's basically annoyed at me, and I'm equally annoyed at them. All I want to do is go to my room and shut the door. But, of course, it's Sunday dinner, and no one's allowed to sit that one out.

Joy.

If the team's not stopping some criminal mastermind, we get together every Sunday evening for a group dinner. Dad started the tradition before Grace and I were even born. He calls it team-building. From the hours of dish duty I'm stuck with, I call it a violation of child labor laws.

When dinner prep gets going, the Galley turns into a three-ring circus on steroids. Mom and Master Mime do all the cooking. Between Mom's telekinesis, and Master Mime's magic, there's always pots, pans and food products flying all over the place. Blue Bolt sets the table, zipping back and forth in the blink of an eye. Makeshift creates desserts, porting in exotic ingredients from who knows where. Dad chases everyone around with a dustpan and broom, advocating kitchen safety. Grace and I pitch in where needed. But poor Shadow Hawk has the worst job of all. He tries to keep TechnocRat's paws out of the kitchen until dinner is served.

With so much action, someone inevitably ends up wearing part the meal before it starts. Tonight was my turn. So, after I peel a fistful of spaghetti off my shirt, we're finally ready to sit down.

That's when Grace pokes the bear.

"Brother, dear," she says ever so sweetly. "Can you please pass the garlic bread? That is, if you're not too wiped out after your adventure."

I stare her down like a lion at an antelope convention. "Of course, dear sister," I answer, shoving the bread basket into her hand. "It's no trouble at all."

"So, there's one thing I still don't understand," she

says, chewing with her mouth open. "How did you manage to defeat this villain who was so powerful he captured the entire Ominous Eight all on your own?"

"I already told you," I say, digging into my spaghetti. "I didn't defeat him. Somehow he teleported away. Trust me, if that didn't happen, he would've crushed me. After all, he *is* Meta-Taker's son."

Suddenly, I hear forks clanging on plates. I look up to see that everyone's stopped eating.

They're all looking at me.

"I did mention that, didn't I?"

"What do you mean, he's Meta-Taker's son?" Mom asks.

"Well," I say, "he told me Meta-Taker was his dad. I mean, he looked just like Meta-Taker. But a lot younger."

"Why didn't you mention this before?" Dad asks sternly.

Uh-oh.

"I ... I thought I did," I say. "I mean, so much was happening when you got there. I thought I told somebody. I mean, I told one of you guys, right?"

But all I get back are blank stares.

Oh boy.

"Whoops," I say. "Sorry."

"*Whoops?*" Mom repeats. "*Sorry?* Not only were you impulsive, reckless, and obstinate ..."

There's that word again.

"... but you also forgot to mention the most

important part—that he's the son of the most powerful Meta we ever faced? Elliott what's gotten into you?"

"I-I don't know," I say. "I guess it slipped my mind when you grounded me."

"Yeah," says Grace. "Along with your brain."

"Stuff it!" I snap.

"You stuff it!" Grace fires back.

"Enough," says Mom. "Both of you."

Shadow Hawk stands up. "I think we should head back down to that warehouse and look around some more. There may be some clues we missed."

The rest of the team rises in agreement. Grace shoots me a sly smile. I'm all alone at the table, except for Mom who hangs back for a minute.

She looks at me. "Elliott, why don't you clear the table, and go to your room. We'll talk more when I get back."

"Awesome," I say, "I've been trying to go to my room for hours."

"And no shenanigans," she adds, before leaving.

I throw my hands in the air. Yep, that's me, Captain Shenanigans. I put everything away, grab the basket of garlic bread, and head for my room.

I mean, c'mon! It was an innocent mistake.

You can't tell me they haven't made mistakes before. Granted, I've made a whole bunch of mistakes in a really short timeframe. But I'm a kid. I'm supposed to make mistakes!

I stop in the middle of the hallway, listening for the pitter-patter of furry feet, but don't hear anything. I guess Dog-Gone isn't coming either. That's fine. I'd rather be alone anyway. Besides, he hogs the bed.

I slam the door behind me, flop down on my bed, and stare at the ceiling. If I'm stuck here for a month I'm going to go nuts. Maybe I can create a hologram or a paper mache version of myself. Then I can go out and live in the real world while my doppelganger gets stuck in here serving out my punishment. Yeah, wouldn't that be grand.

Just wonderful.

BOOM!

Suddenly, the whole room tilts right, throwing me off my bed. Everything not nailed down to a surface crashes to the floor. Then the room levels off again.

What the ... ?

"Waystation breached!" blares the Meta Monitor. "Repeat, Waystation breached! Automatic emergency response system activated! Repeat, automatic emergency response system activated!"

I spring from the floor. Did that just say 'breached?' That can only mean one thing—the Waystation's been invaded!

Suddenly, I feel really hot, beads of sweat trickle down my forehead. How is that even possible? I mean, we're hundreds of miles from Earth. Who could possibly board the Waystation?

I run to the porthole. From my window, I have a partial view of the Hanger. I look outside and do a double take. To my astonishment, attached to the end of the Hanger is some kind of a ship!

It's silver and sleek looking, with a long cylindrical body, and a narrow tower jutting up from its center. Thin, fins run along it's sides, and it's capped at the rear by large, powerful-looking jets.

How did it get through our sensors without being detected? That shouldn't be possible!

But, now's not the time to worry about that.

Someone's on the Waystation!

I need to think. I can either stay here and wait to get whacked, or I can try to make it to a Freedom Ferry and get out of here.

Then, I remember Dog-Gone! He's alone out there!

I dig through my closet, grab a baseball bat, and head for the hallway.

Immediately, I've got problems.

The residential wing is cut off by a thick, steel barrier. This must be one of the emergency response actions the Meta Monitor executed. Basically, all it serves to do is keep me trapped like a sitting duck until whoever's here comes to find me. I can't let that happen.

Fortunately, I know a workaround.

"Override ZY78840C," I yell.

The barrier retracts into the ceiling. It's a good thing I proofread all of TechnocRat's manuals. I've got to find that mutt and get out of here.

Now where would I be hiding if I were a dog?

Of course!

I sprint up the West Wing staircase and hit the most logical place possible—the Galley.

I enter to find something I'm totally not expecting.

Sitting at the end of the table, eating our leftover spaghetti, is a monkey. He's black, and furry, and absolutely stuffing his face.

Our eyes meet, but he keeps shoveling in as many noodles as possible. He doesn't even react to me.

Gross.

Whoever it is that's invaded the Waystation owns a pet that's more interested in raiding my refrigerator than Dog-Gone. I have no clue who this monkey belongs to, but that person must be here somewhere. I scan the room, but there's no one else around.

And speaking of Dog-Gone, I don't see him anywhere. I've got to find that flea bag before I take off. I just can't leave him here to be captured. Or worse ...

I'm about to head out, when ...

"Excuse me," comes a gravelly voice from behind.

I turn, baseball bat fully extended. My eyes dart back and forth, but there's no one here. It's just me and the monkey.

"I said, excuse me," comes the voice again.

"Who's there!" I yell. "Come on out!"

"Are you blind?" comes the voice again. Out of the

corner of my eye, I see the monkey waving at me with his long, hairy arm.

No. Freaking. Way.

"Ah, yes, now you see me," says the monkey. "I was a bit worried for a moment." He stares at me with his large, brown eyes. As I look closer at his face and ears, I realize he's a chimpanzee.

"You did this?" I ask. "Who are you?"

The chimp picks up a long noodle and slurps it into his mouth. "Oh, this is so good. I haven't had food from my world in such a long, long time. You wouldn't happen to have tabasco sauce, would you? I used to love tabasco sauce."

"Um, no," I answer. "Look, I don't have time for this right now."

"No, you don't," says the chimp. "I suppose you've been invaded, haven't you?"

"I'll ask you one more time," I say, waving the bat. "Who are you?"

"Very well," says the chimp. "They call me Leo. Now perhaps you can answer a question for me. Are you Elliott Harkness?"

The sound of my name coming from the mouth of a monkey takes me aback for a second. "Um, yes," I answer.

"The Orb Master?" asks Leo.

Orb Master? What the heck does this monkey know about the Orb of Oblivion?

"I ... I guess so," I answer.

"Excellent," says Leo.

Suddenly, I hear a THWIP, and feel a sharp pain in my left leg. There's a small puff of smoke floating up from beneath Leo's table.

I look down to see a dart sticking out of my leg!

Then, I look back at Leo, who's busy slurping up another noodle.

And everything goes dark.

Meta Profile

The Ominous Eight

Die-Abolical
Class: Super-Intellect
Meta: ■■■■

Frightmare
Class: Magic
Meta: ■■■■

Think Tank
Class: Psychic
Meta: ■■■■

The Atomic Rage
Class: Energy Manipulator
Meta: ■■■■■

Airess
Class: Energy Manipulator
Meta: ■■■■

Rundown
Class: Super-Speed
Meta: ■■

Back Breaker
Class: Super-Strength
Meta: ■■■■

Fire Fiend
Class: Meta-morph
Meta: ■■■■

FOUR

I THINK I'VE BEEN ABDUCTED BY ALIENS

"We should kill him," comes a girl's voice.

Well, that didn't sound neighborly, especially since I suspect whoever said it is talking about me! I only regained consciousness seconds ago, and I have no clue where I am, or what's happening around me.

Whatever that monkey hit me with was pretty potent, because my eyelids feel like they're stuck together with crazy glue. Fortunately, my ears are working just fine. So, for the moment, I figure my best bet is to play cadaver and collect intel.

Not that I could do anything about my situation even if I wanted to. I'm lying face up on a cold table and my wrists and ankles are locked down tight. I hear loud shuffling to my right and then—

"Kill the Orb Master?" comes a raspy-voiced response. "Gemini, you're insane." I know that voice. It's that monkey that shot me—Leo.

"I'm not insane," Gemini replies. "I'm practical. Everyone in the universe is looking for him, which means everyone in the universe is now looking for us."

Um, what does she mean by *everyone in the universe?*

"We'll never survive an onslaught," comes a new voice—female, but deeper.

"We won't have to, Taurus," comes yet another voice, this time confident and male. "Don't forget, we're in the Ghost Ship. No one can track us."

"Right, Scorpio," says Taurus. "You be sure to tell them that when your molecules are scattered all over the galaxy. Besides, look at him—so puny and weak. I think we jacked the wrong human."

Ouch—now I'm captured *and* offended.

"We need answers," Scorpio says. "When is he going to wake up?"

"I'll stick him with a stimulant," says Leo. "That'll get him up."

Wait? What? "Hold your horses, Curious George!" I yell. "I'm up! Don't stick me with anything!"

With all of my might, I force my eyes open. Everything's blurry for a few seconds, and then my vision begins to clear. To my surprise, standing over me are a bunch of ... teenagers?

Alien teenagers—about my age.

They're staring at me warily, like I could bust out of these shackles, and steal their lunch money.

If they only knew ...

I take in my captors.

In the front is a pretty girl with green skin, orange eyes, and two antenna stalks poking through her long, black hair. She's wearing a bodysuit that's color-split down the middle—one half blue and the other half red. On her belt is a symbol that looks like a mathematical pi sign. Guessing by her irritated expression, she must be Gemini.

Standing behind her is the largest girl I've ever seen. She has a round face with strange blue markings all over it. Her hair is pulled up in a samurai-like bun. Her arms are ripped, and she's reaching down towards two long swords at her hips—her fingers twitching nervously. On her shoulder plates is a symbol of a creature with gigantic, violent-looking horns. I'm pegging her as Taurus.

On the other side is a red-skinned dude with cables running in and out of various parts of his body. He's staring me down through a pair of blue goggles. He looks wiry, but that's not the part that worries me. Behind his back I see a large mechanical-looking tail waving menacingly back and forth. He's got to be Scorpio.

And finally, crouching in front of him is my old pal, Leo. He's brandishing a gigantic syringe with the business end pointed at my leg. There's a spaghetti noodle dangling from the fur beneath his chin. Nice.

"Well," I say, "this has been fun, but if you don't mind I'm kind of tired. So, how about we swing by my place and drop me off?"

"Sorry," says Leo. "But you're not going anywhere."

"Enough stalling," says Scorpio, "Tell us, where is the Orb of Oblivion?"

So the chimp wasn't lying. This really *is* about the Orb.

Okay, so what the heck do I do now? If I tell them I blew up the Orb along with a Skelton warship they'll probably kill me on the spot. But, if I make up some story about the Orb being hidden or lost or something, maybe they'll keep me around for a while—or maybe they'll kill me on the spot anyway. Decisions, decisions.

They're staring at me intently, hanging on whatever I'm about to say. Then I realize I've got something they want. Maybe I'm actually in the power position here.

So, I get bold.

"Why should I tell you?"

Taurus grabs a metal bar, rips it off the wall, and snaps it in two.

"Hey!" Leo shouts. "Don't break my medi-wing!"

"Okay, I see your point," I say. "But I really can't think straight when I'm all pinned down like this. The blood is flowing away from my brain and I think my feet are asleep."

I watch their eyes drift to Scorpio.

Now I know who's in charge.

"Unshackle him," says Scorpio.

"What," says Gemini. "Are you nuts?"

"Scorpio, please—," Taurus starts.

"I said, unshackle him," Scorpio repeats firmly.

Leo hops on the table and releases my arms and legs.

"Thanks," I say, rubbing my sore wrists. "Now we're getting somew—"

Suddenly, Scorpio's tail is inches from my face. It looks like a red battering ram perched on a slinky. Then, the tip turns bright orange and starts radiating heat. It feels like my skin is melting!

"Let's come to an understanding," he says. "We need something from you, the Orb of Oblivion. And you need something from us, your life. So, in order for you to get what you want, you're going to give us what we want. Is that clear?"

The temperature coming off his tail is so intense, sweat starts pouring down my face.

Its impressive. But I have powers too.

"I hear you," I say. "But I think it's only fair if we start from an even playing field." I concentrate, and bathe him with my negation energy. I hope this works! Seconds later, his tail snuffs out.

Scorpio looks stunned.

"Scorpio!" Taurus says, moving forward.

"Wait, Taurus," says Gemini. "He has power."

Than it hits me. Scorpio? Taurus? Gemini?

"Hang on," I say. "Aren't your names, like, the signs of the zodiac? But aren't there twelve signs?"

"We *were* twelve," says Gemini, sadly.

Then, I realize there's only four of them. I look at Leo. "Hey, and isn't Leo supposed to be a lion? You know he's a monkey, right?"

Leo raises a fist.

"Leo, no!" Gemini orders.

"So, where are the rest of you?" I ask.

"Pisces and Sagittarius are piloting the vessel," Gemini answers. "Aries ... disappeared. The rest are dead."

They all look down. It's quiet for a few seconds.

"Look, I'm sorry to hear that," I say. "And I'd love to help out in any way that doesn't involve my captivity. But, I really have no idea what I'm doing here. Or what you want the Orb for."

Gemini looks over to Scorpio who nods his approval.

"We're the Zodiac," she starts. "A band of survivors—vigilantes—bonded in a shared quest to destroy the one who annihilated our worlds."

"Annihilated?" The words shock me for a minute. "Y-you mean your world was ... destroyed?"

"Not world, Orb Master," Gemini says. "Worlds. My planet was called Gallron. It was beautiful, with bright purple skies, and rolling seas. At night, the moons would glow, illuminating the seven kingdoms filled with a peaceful people. But now ... now it's gone. If I wasn't sent into space on a scientific expedition moments before it happened, then I'd be gone as well."

"And it's the same for me," says Taurus. "I hail from Pollux, a planet covered with mountains and forests. The weather was harsh, but the people hardy. I was on orbital patrol that fateful day. There was going to be a celebration. But it never happened."

I look over at Scorpio, but he's silent. I can see his pain through his goggles.

"And what about you?" I ask Leo. "Didn't you say you were from Earth?"

"I did," says Leo, breathing out deeply. "This may be hard for you to believe, but ..."

KABOOM!

Suddenly, the ship turns upside down, sending all of us crashing into the ceiling. Then, the ship rights itself, and we smash to the floor. Leo is lying on top of me, his tail planted squarely in my mouth.

I push him away, spitting out a mouthful of fur. "What was that?" I ask.

Suddenly, I hear clopping, like a giant horse is racing through the ship. Just then, a bearded figure appears in the doorway. At first, I think it's a man, but then I realize it's a muscular kid's upper body attached to the lower half of some kind of six-legged creature! He stares at me with his emerald eyes.

"Sagittarius!" Scorpio says. "What's going on?"

"We were hit with a concussion blast! That was only a warning shot," Sagittarius says. "It's a warship. They say if we don't land immediately, they'll destroy us."

"Impossible!" Scorpio exclaims. "The Ghost Ship can't be tracked!"

"Told you," Taurus says. "What are we going to do now!"

"Where's the closest landing point?" Scorpio asks.

"There's a small moon below us," Sagittarius says. "But we aren't faster than the warship."

"Whoa!" I say panicked. "Wait a minute. If the Skelton find out I'm on board, they'll kill me for what I've done!"

"Oh, they're not Skelton," Sagittarius says. "They're much, much worse."

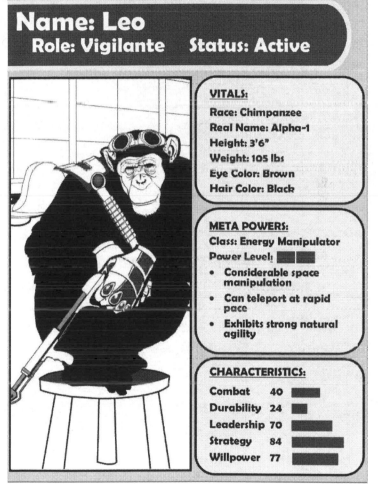

Meta Profile

Name: Leo
Role: Vigilante   Status: Active

VITALS:

Race: Chimpanzee
Real Name: Alpha-1
Height: 3'6"
Weight: 105 lbs
Eye Color: Brown
Hair Color: Black

META POWERS:

Class: Energy Manipulator
Power Level: ▆▆▆

- Considerable space manipulation
- Can teleport at rapid pace
- Exhibits strong natural agility

CHARACTERISTICS:

Combat	40	▆
Durability	24	▆
Leadership	70	▆
Strategy	84	▆
Willpower	77	▆

FIVE

I GET CAUGHT IN A TUG OF WAR

"**U**m, what do you mean by *worse* than the Skelton?"

Despite my overactive imagination, I simply can't fathom anything worse than the Skelton. From everything I've seen, the Skelton Emperor will do whatever it takes—and I mean *what-ever it takes*—to rule the universe. So, who could possibly be worse than that?

"That's a *Dhoom* warship," Gemini whispers, like it's obvious to anyone with half a brain.

We're now standing on the main bridge of the Ghost Ship, practically nose-to-nose with the most impressive spacecraft I've seen outside of a Star Wars movie. The ship is just enormous, fanning out from the center, its massive circular body dwarfing it's smaller, spherical cockpit. Two thin wings extend out from the sides, seemingly going on for miles, every square inch covered by some weapon that's pointed directly at us. The monolith drifts slowly forwards, closing in for the kill.

I wait for Gemini to clue me in further, but apparently, the fact that it's a Dhoom warship seems to be explanation enough. "Sorry," I say, "I know I'm the new guy here, but who exactly are the Dhoom again?"

"Seriously?" Gemini says. "Don't they have schools on your planet? On Dhoom, there's no government, no laws, no justice—the only currency is strength. Their entire society is split into fiefdoms, each ruled by a crime lord looking to expand his empire by conquering worlds and enslaving whole civilizations. To rise to power on Dhoom, you don't ask, you take what you want."

I suddenly wonder if Dog Gone is part Dhoom?

"Okay," I say. "I get that's bad, but how are they worse than the Skelton?"

Gemini looks me square in the eyes. "If you're captured by Skelton, they'll kill you. If you're captured by Dhoom, you'll beg them to kill you. Is that clear?"

"Crystal," I say.

"Scorpio!" calls a small girl wearing a red, scaled costume. She has black, spikey hair, and tiny, gill-like flaps on the sides of her neck that open and close. Based on the process of elimination, she must be Pisces. She pushes a few buttons at the controls and says, "We're being hailed on communications frequency X12. They want to talk."

"Open the channel," Scorpio says grimly.

Suddenly, the image of a man appears on the monitor. The first thing I notice is his blue skin. Then, there's his size. Even though he's projecting from the chest up, I can tell by his thick neck and broad shoulders that he's absolutely ginormous. Finally, there's his yellow eyes with elliptical, almost cat-like pupils—which only grow larger when they land on me.

His lips curl into a disturbing smile, exposing razor sharp fangs. "What a pleasant surprise" he says. "I had thought you were just another smuggler ship violating interstellar trade laws. But it appears your cargo is far more valuable than I ever could have imagined."

"Who are you?" Scorpio asks.

"My true name will hold no meaning for you," the man says. "But, you will know me best as the Overlord."

Gemini gasps. I catch the rest of the Zodiac shooting worried glances at one another.

Scorpio crosses his arms. "Yeah, we've heard of you. Now what do you want?"

"Originally, I wanted your ship, I haven't seen many custom-builds like it," the Overlord says. "But now I will take something of far greater value—the Orb Master. Only I thought he would be more … impressive."

I sense this is going to be a theme.

"Transport him to my ship," the Overlord continues, "and I will consider letting the rest of you live. You have one minute to decide." Then, the communication cuts off and the screen goes blank.

Everyone turns my way.

Suddenly, I feel like the anchor on a hot air balloon.

"You're not going to give me to that guy," I say. "Are you?"

Gemini points at me. "Seize him!"

Before I can react, Taurus grabs my arms. I try pulling away, but she's way too strong.

"Wait!" Leo says. "We can't do it."

"Listen to the monkey," I plead. "He's got good ideas."

"You heard him," Gemini says, pointing back to the screen. "That's the Overlord! You know, the intergalactic crime boss of all crime bosses. The pirate that traffics illegal slaves across the universe. The torturer that experiments on beings for his own amusement. I say we dump this annoying kid now, before it's too late."

"Annoying is a little harsh," I mutter. "Pesky, maybe, but annoying?"

"Listen," Leo says. "If the Overlord gets his mitts on the Orb of Oblivion we're as good as dead anyway. I know this isn't popular, but this kid knows where the Orb is. If we just turn him over, then all of the universe is lost."

"Leo's right," Scorpio says, stepping forward. "If we're going to avenge our worlds, then we need to stand and fight."

There's a long moment of silence. It's clearly tense.

Until, finally, Gemini relents. "Fine. We must fight for the lives we've lost."

Reluctantly, Taurus lets me go.

Gemini turns towards me. "But, you do know where the Orb is, right? We're counting on you."

I look at their hopeful faces staring at me—like a gang of ragamuffins begging for a free meal. I feel bad. I mean, despite the odds, they're actually willing to fight for me. Maybe even die for me. But, the truth is, I don't have what they're looking for.

The Orb is gone. Destroyed. Kaput.

I can't let them risk their lives without knowing the truth. "So, here's the funny thing. I ... kind of ... well, you might say, I ... um ... I ..."

"What?" Gemini says impatiently. "You what?"

"Blew up the Orb with a Skelton Blood Bringer ship somewhere in outer space," I finish quickly.

"What?" Taurus says.

"You idiot!" Gemini screams. "Do you know what you've done!"

"Well," I answer, "it sort of seemed like a good idea at the time. I mean, I didn't need the orb anymore, and I wanted to make sure those guys never returned to destroy Earth. So, I told the Orb to self-destruct."

Gemini shakes her fist at me. "I'm gonna make you self-destruct!"

"Hold it," Scorpio says. "You *told* the Orb of Oblivion to blow itself up?"

"Please, stop," Gemini says, her head in her hands. "I'm losing brain cells every time he speaks."

"The Overlord's calling back!" Pisces yells from the helm. "We need a decision!"

Gemini looks at Scorpio, who looks at Leo, who shoots back an expression I can't read.

"Patch him through," Scorpio says.

Just then, the Overlord reappears. "So, have you chosen to live, or to die?"

Scorpio takes a deep breath.

Well, it was an interesting life while it lasted.

"Our sincere apologies, Overlord," Scorpio says, "But we've decided to keep him."

What? Really?

The Overlord smiles. "I was hoping you would say that. Prepare for landing."

Suddenly, our ship jerks downward with incredible force. My feet leave the ground, and I slam hard into the ceiling. Instinctively, I curl into a ball, shielding myself from flying cabin equipment, flailing body parts, and a screeching chimpanzee.

It feels like we're on a permanent downhill rollercoaster ride—pinned to the ceiling by unrelenting antigravity. Stars zip past the windshield, but I know we're the ones moving at incredible speed. The Overlord must be forcing our ship down with some kind of propulsion beam! And when we land it's not going to be—

CRASH!

The collision is bone-rattling!

We're jolted from the ceiling back to the floor. My head bounces off something large and soft, which turns out to be Sagittarius' rump.

Miraculously, everyone seems okay. Badly bruised, but okay.

"Quick," Scorpio commands, "Activate your stream suits."

I watch the team push the Zodiac symbols on their uniforms. Suddenly, they're wrapped in a clear film that flexes in and out with their breathing.

Just then—with a loud POP—the Ghost Ship's exterior hatch opens. But I'm not wearing a stream suit! If I can't breathe in this atmosphere, I'll die!

Something slaps me hard on my chest. I look down to find Pisces standing there, a disc attached to my costume. She smiles, and then pokes it.

Suddenly, I'm wrapped head-to-toe in a cellophane-like substance. I feel like a cucumber heading into the fridge, but at least I can breathe!

"Thanks," I say.

"Just don't die in it," she says. "It costs a fortune to clean."

Leo waves his dart gun at me, "Stay here and don't do anything stupid."

I follow orders as the Zodiac file out of the Ghost Ship, and close the hatch behind them.

The next thing I know, it sounds like World War III out there. The way the Ghost Ship is positioned, I can't see any of the action, so I run through my options.

If the Overlord wins, I'll become his captive, and based on what I've learned, that's not a good thing. If the Zodiac win, I'm still their captive, but now they know I don't have the Orb. So, that pretty much makes me expendable.

What to do?

Suddenly, I see a half-man, half-horse fly past the windshield. I scramble over to the hatch, throw it open, and peek outside.

The scene is pure crazy-town.

The Zodiac are standing back to back, trying to hold off hundreds of advancing Dhoom soldiers. I don't see how this could possibly end well.

But what happens next shocks me.

Scorpio uses his tail to generate a massive bolt of energy, blasting a clear path through the heart of the enemy. Taurus pounds the earth with her giant fists, causing an earthquake that topples a battalion of soldiers. Leo is teleporting all over the place, punching out Dhoom warriors one by one. Pisces is flying gracefully through space, creating tornado-like dust storms that lift up dozens of soldiers and send them miles away.

And Gemini ... well, let's just say I do a double take. To my right is a ten-foot tall version of Gemini in red—and to my left is another ten-foot tall Gemini, but in blue!

The Zodiac have Meta-powers!

But, there's way too many Dhoom to hold back. I see Pisces get nailed with a boulder, Taurus and Scorpio are quickly over-run, and Leo looks like he's been captured. This is going south fast!

I should get out of here. I should figure out how to pilot the Ghost Ship and save myself. I don't owe these guys anything. I mean, they kidnapped me!

"Help!," Gemini cries.

The Overlord is standing over Blue Gemini, his arms folded across his chest, while she's being pushed into the ground like there's an anvil on top of her! Then I realize it wasn't any propulsion beam that forced our ship down, it was the Overlord himself! He can manipulate gravity!

"Stop!" Red Gemini screams. But she's captured by Dhoom soldiers, helpless to save her twin.

Despite everything that's happened, I can't run away when someone's in trouble. I guess that's why I'm petitioning so hard to be a superhero.

I jump from the hatch, and run towards the Overlord. "Release her!" I demand.

But the Overlord just stares at me with his electric eyes. "Ah," he says, "the Orb Master finally shows himself. I know several customers who will pay quite handsomely for your hide—dead or alive. So, let's end this, shall we?"

He raises his eyebrows, and Blue Gemini is pushed deeper into the ground! He's going to bury her alive!

"No!" Red Gemini yells.

I haven't used my powers around this many Metas since I messed up the mission with the Destruction Crew. I don't want to accidently negate the Zodiac's powers, but what other choice do I have? I focus deeply on the Overlord, and let my powers fly.

Suddenly, Blue Gemini emerges from the ground, and the Gemini twins hurtle towards one another, merging into one with violent force. Fused back together, Gemini collapses to the ground. I must have negated her powers! Which means I saved her, but I still don't have control over my own powers.

The Overlord stares at his hands. "Impressive. You have eliminated my powers, but you have not eliminated me."

He takes a step towards me, when he's suddenly engulfed in a strange orange energy.

No way. Not again.

"What is this?" he says. "Release me!"

The energy lifts him off the ground.

"What is happeni—"

And then, just like Siphon, he's gone!

I look around to find the Dhoom soldiers in shock.

I realize this is our chance. Maybe our only chance. I need to bluff like there's no tomorrow!

"Let go of my friends!" I command. "I ... I am the Orb Master! Release them, or I'll do the same to you!"

Without their leader, the Dhoom look at one

another, unsure if they should fight, or run.

I raise my arms threateningly. "Now!"

They push their Zodiac captives into the center.

I spin, pointing at them all. "Now return to your ship. Go!"

The Dhoom retreat, scrambling over one another to get back to their warship.

Gemini is still on the ground, breathing hard. "Thank you, Orb Master. You saved my life."

"No problem," I say. "And you can call me Epic Zero. Or Elliott if you want. I'm really not feeling the Orb Master thing."

"Did you do that?" Gemini says, her eyes wide.

I could lie to her, but I'm not sure what that buys me. "No," I say. "That wasn't me. But I've seen it happen before. So that's twice now."

"So have we," Scorpio says. "That's how we lost Aries—our greatest fighter. He disappeared right before our eyes in that same strange energy."

"Great," I say, "so what the heck's going on?"

Scorpio scratches his head. "I don't know. But I may know someone who does."

Gemini glares at him "No, Scorpio. He's a madman."

"I know" Scorpio says. "Which is exactly why he may have the answer."

Meta Profile

Name: The Overlord
Role: Dictator   Status: Active

VITALS:

Race: Dhoom
Real Name: Unknown
Height: 6'9"
Weight: 546 lbs
Eye Color: Yellow
Hair Color: Bald

META POWERS:

Class: Energy Manipulator
Power Level:

- **Extreme gravity manipulation**
- **Can increase mass or density of objects or beings**
- **Can also negate gravity**

CHARACTERISTICS:

Combat	95
Durability	66
Leadership	91
Strategy	100
Willpower	100

SIX

I HAVE QUITE A REPUTATION

You know it's been a strange day when you're hanging with a bunch of aliens, and *you* feel like the weird one.

After the Dhoom departed, Scorpio went right to work fixing the Ghost Ship. The good news is that despite our forced crash-landing on this nameless moon, the ship is salvageable. The bad news is that I still have no clue how to get back home.

I watch Scorpio detach cables from his body and plug them into different parts of the ship. It's like he's talking directly to the wiring itself! I bet TechnocRat wished he could do that.

I pick Scorpio's brain as he works. He explains how the Ghost Ship is invisible to conventional radar. It's designed to fly in 'pocket space,' which is a dimension of space that exists within traditional space, but is hidden from view. The only way I can get my mind around it is to think about Dog-Gone when he's invisible, and there's no trail of crumbs to track him down.

"I just can't figure out how the Overlord found us," Scorpio says. "We should have been undetectable."

"Maybe it's Leo," I offer. "You guys ever give that chimp a bath? I don't want to be rude, but he smells like—"

"Hey," Scorpio interjects. "It happened right after you used your powers on me. Maybe when you negated my powers, you negated the cloaking powers of the Ghost Ship?"

I look at him skeptically. "How's that possible? My powers only work on living things?"

"I don't know," Scorpio says. "But let me give it some thought. There has to be an answer."

Speaking of answers, there's one thing that's been bugging me. How did the Zodiac find me in the first place? I mean, there are billions of people on Earth. Finding me had to be like finding the proverbial needle in a haystack. I ask Scorpio the question, but he doesn't give me a straight answer. All he says is to ask Leo. Then he tells me to get ready for lift-off.

Leo? Why Leo?

I climb inside the Ghost Ship. There's no sign of Leo anywhere, so I hook myself in. After a few minutes, we take off.

I try to make sense of what's happened. The Zodiac want the Orb of Oblivion to take down whoever's responsible for destroying their worlds. But I don't know anything about this guy, or how they planned to use the Orb once they had it. I look for someone to talk to, but everyone's busy. Everyone, that is, except for Gemini.

She's sitting in the corner with her head resting on her knees. She's definitely had a rough time of it. But, if it wasn't for me, she'd have lost half her body. So, I figure she's my best bet. I unclick myself and make my way over.

"Hey," I say, sitting down next to her.

"Hey," she says. "Thanks again for saving me."

"No problem. I'm sure you would've done the same for me."

She looks at me, her eyebrows raised.

"Okay, maybe not. Look, I've got to be honest here. I have no clue what's going on. I don't know why you kidnapped me. I mean, I know you want the Orb of Oblivion, but why? What's this all about?"

Gemini looks at me like I have three heads. "What's this all about? Over 20 billion people lived on my world. They were artists, musicians, performers. All of them had the ability to split into two. Do you know what it's like to hear the screams of 40 billion souls? That's what this is all about."

"Sorry, I didn't mean it like that," I say. "What I'm trying to find out is who did this to you? To all of you?"

"Ravager," she says with disgust.

"Who's Ravager?" I ask.

"Ravager is not a *who*, it's a *what*—a giant, nebulous cosmic entity that consumes the life force of entire planets to sustain itself. It's uncontrollable. Unstoppable. It travels across galaxies, and wipes out solar systems. It destroyed my world, and one day it will destroy yours too. Unless, of course, you can stop it."

"*Me?*" I say, "How can *I* stop something that eats planets for breakfast?"

Gemini crosses her legs. "You're the mighty Orb Master, shouldn't you know?"

I rub my face. "Some mighty Orb Master I am. I don't even have an orb."

"So, we're basically screwed," she says.

"Yeah," I say. "That pretty much sums it up."

"Great," she says. "Glad you're on board."

So now this is my fault? Like I knew that I'm supposed to be the savior of the universe. Me, the guy who can't control his own powers. Me, the guy who gets sent to his room after dinner? Well, sorry, but that's utterly ridiculous.

We sit in silence for a few minutes.

"You said you've seen that orange energy before," she says. "The one that swallowed the Overlord."

"Yeah, it happened back on Earth," I say, happy to change the subject. "To this really powerful villain named Siphon. And you said it happened to your teammate?"

"Yeah, a few days ago," Gemini says. "His name was Aries—also powerful. We were in the middle of a battle with a group of Baltian soldiers. The orange energy came, and then suddenly, he vanished. We haven't heard from him since."

My mind starts spinning. I mean, Siphon and the Overlord are major villains. If Aries is equally as strong, then whoever's doing this must be even stronger. But who could that be? I have no idea.

"So, who's this madman that has all the answers?"

"The Watcher," she says. "He's spends all of eternity observing the evolution of the universe."

Eternity? "So, he's like, millions of years old?"

"Billions," Gemini says. "Legends say that in exchange for his immortality, he's sworn not to interfere in the affairs of the universe."

"What kind of tooth fairy is out there handing out immortality?" I ask. "And where do I get in line?"

"Supposedly, it's a one-of-a-kind gift of the universe. But, his gift is also his curse. While he's seen everything that's ever happened since the dawn of time, legends also say he's lost his mind."

"Wonderful," I say. "Can't wait to meet him."

"If he allows it," Gemini says. "No one's safely reached his world in centuries. We'll see him, but only if he wants to see us."

"Strap in!" Pisces orders from the helm. "Watcher World is approaching. Prepare for descent."

I strap myself in, and lean over to look out the front window, but all I see is a giant asteroid belt. There must be hundreds of rocks out there, in all shapes and sizes, smashed together to form an impenetrable wall.

Now I get what Gemini was saying. No one's reaching Watcher World unless the Watcher allows it.

We get closer, but the asteroids aren't budging.

"300 meters," Pisces says.

"Hold steady," Scorpio says coolly.

"200 meters," Pisces says.

Taurus looks at me nervously.

"Hold," Scorpio says, shifting in his chair.

"100 meters," Pisces says, her voice rising sharply.

Those rocks are huge!

"We should turn back," Sagittarius says.

"Hold course!" Scorpio commands.

"50 meters," Pisces says quickly. "Shouldn't we—"

"Hold steady!" Scorpio commands.

"Scorpio!" Gemini shouts. "Are you crazy!"

"10 meters!" Pisces shouts.

A giant asteroid—irregularly shaped and pock-marked—fills the entire windshield. It's not moving!

"Hold!" Scorpio yells.

We're gonna smash into it!

Gemini screams.

I shut my eyes and clutch the arm rests.

But, instead of being obliterated, nothing happens.

I open my eyes to find a ringed, red planet floating in

space.

"W-what happened?" I ask. "Why aren't we space-kill?"

"Because it was an illusion," Scorpio says. "Let's call it a test. We passed."

"Well, thank goodness for that," I say, sliding down in my chair. "But if there's a follow-up exam, I'm calling in sick."

Gemini shakes her head. "It's not that kind of a test. Scorpio, do you know where we'll find him? I mean, that's a whole planet down there."

"Yes," Scorpio says. "According to legend he prefers to be west of the giant crater. I suggest we start there."

"Will do," Pisces says. "Prepare for landing."

We touch down minutes later. Despite the planet appearing red from outer space, the surface seems more purplish in color.

"Stream suits on," Scorpio advises. "As far as I know, no one has reached the surface for centuries. So let's be ready for anything. And remember, when we find the Watcher, let me do all the talking. Is that clear?" For some reason, he's looking at me.

Why do aliens think I always cause the problems?

We exit the Ghost Ship and hit the ground.

The sky is blood red and dotted with black clouds. Stringy, white lightning flashes overhead, occasionally striking the ground with violent results. The terrain is rough and challenging—ranging from tall, jagged rocks to deep, bottomless crevices. We carefully make our way, passing clusters of orange plant-like things swaying gently in the soft breeze.

After what seems like hours, Taurus has had it. She plops down on a rock, rubbing her feet. "We need to stop. I'm getting blisters."

I take a seat next to her, my own feet throbbing. It seems hopeless, like we've been walking in circles.

Suddenly, Sagittarius rears up on his hind legs and points towards the sky. "There," he says.

We look up to see a white object sitting high atop a mountain. Bingo! But how are we going to get way up there?

"Stand together," Pisces says. "And stay close."

From what I can tell, Pisces is an energy manipulator who can control the density of air molecules. We form a tight circle around her, joining hands. Pisces concentrates, creating a platform of air that lifts us off the ground and all the way to the top of the mountain.

We step off onto the summit to find a large, white structure that looks like a Greek temple—square in shape with wide marble columns. At its center is a giant chair with a large, robed figure sitting in it.

The Watcher!

"Remember," Scorpio says. "I'll do the talking."

As we approach, I try calculating how old this guy is. Gemini said he's been around since the beginning of time, so if the known universe is something like ten or twelve billion years old, then this dude has had loads of birthdays. I mean, what do you get for a guy who's seen everything?

We climb the marble steps, Scorpio in the lead.

The Watcher's head is down, like he's sleeping. In his right hand is a thin, golden staff. I study his bald head, expecting to see tons of liver spots or something, but it's totally smooth.

As we reach the top step, we look at one another, unsure of what to do next. We're here because Scorpio thinks the Watcher may have the answer to what's happening with these vanishing people, including Aries. I guess if you've seen everything you can solve lots of mysteries. Hopefully, this guy never misses a trick.

Scorpio clears his throat, about to speak, when—

"Bring me the Orb Master," comes a deep voice.

Oh, geez.

Suddenly, The Watcher lifts his head—revealing a surprisingly young-looking face.

But that's not what really gets my attention.

His eyes—they're completely white.

The Watcher is ... blind?

Meta Profile

Name: Gemini
Role: Vigilante   Status: Active

VITALS:

Race: Gallronian
Real Name: Steva Duon 12
Height: 5'2"
Weight: 108 lbs
Eye Color: Orange
Hair Color: Black

META POWERS:

Class: Meta-morph
Power Level: ▇▇

- Can split into two identical bodies
- Each body can Increase in size up to 10 feet
- Retains experiences each divided self obtains

CHARACTERISTICS:

Combat	45	▇▇
Durability	21	▇
Leadership	72	▇▇▇
Strategy	75	▇▇▇
Willpower	89	▇▇▇▇

SEVEN

I WANT TO HURL MYSELF OFF A CLIFF

"**B**ring forth the Orb Master!" the Watcher commands.

You ever have a weird dream where you're called to the Principal's office, but have no clue what for?

Well, that's exactly how I'm feeling—except magnified a gazillion times.

Even though he can't see me, the Watcher turns his head in my direction—like he senses me standing behind the Zodiac.

"Bring him to me," the Watcher demands.

The alien teens part nervously, giving me a clear path straight to the Watcher. So much for Scorpio doing all the talking! Other than jumping off the cliff to my death, I have no choice but to step to the front of the class.

It's not until I'm standing in front of the Watcher that I realize how enormous he is. Maybe it's because he's sitting down, but I'm guessing he's at least ten feet tall standing at full height. There's a faint, white glow radiating from his body, making him seem almost heavenly. I'm still shocked that for a dude who's billions of years old, there's not a single wrinkle anywhere on his face. If I could bottle that formula I'd be the richest guy on earth.

I stand awkwardly for what seems like an eternity. I don't know if I should start talking or wait for him. And then—

"Why did you destroy the Orb of Oblivion?" he bellows.

I refrain from wetting myself.

Honestly, I'm not sure what to say. "I, um, thought it was the best idea at the time?" I squeak out.

"Then you are a fool," he responds. "You have destroyed the one agent capable of saving the universe."

Okay, I don't care who this is. I'm getting sick and tired of being called a fool over this Orb thing.

"Look, I may have been a bit rash," I say, "but, the Orb didn't exactly come with a return address."

"You are flippant," the Watcher says. "I sense that you have no remorse for what you have done. The Orb was a tool to be used for good, not a piece of trash to be so recklessly discarded."

Wait, what?

The Orb is a tool for good?

That doesn't jive with anything I know.

I mean, K'ami died to keep the Orb out the hands of her own Skelton people.

I distinctly remember her describing the Orb as a parasite that preyed on its host's most selfish desires. She said it was a living entity of great power that would only be used for death and destruction. I mean, it was purposely placed on a remote planet at the far end of the galaxy so no one would ever find it. How can that possibly be a tool for good?

Something's not adding up.

I look into the Watcher's white eyes and wonder how much he really can see. I mean, Gemini did call him a madman. So, is he really this great observer of life, or is he just a big fraud?

I decide to test the waters.

"With all due respect, Mr. Watcher," I say. "But that's a complete load of crock."

I hear gasps from behind me.

"Elliott," Gemini whispers. "What are you doing?"

"Don't worry," I whisper back. "I've got this."

Her jaw goes slack.

"First of all," I say, "if you really *can* see everything, as my good friends here believe, then you'd know that before the Orb got into my hands, it was stolen by the Skelton Emperor who wanted to take over the entire universe. And second, if it wasn't for me and my friends, we'd all be toast by now. So, for somebody named the Watcher, I'm a little surprised by your lack of clarity on this one."

The Watcher's face turns dark.

"Oh, no he didn't," Gemini whispers behind me.

I feel someone pulling my shoulder from behind.

But I press on. "In fact, I'm guessing you can't see more than a few feet in front of your face. Can you?"

Scorpio grabs my arm. "Time to go, hot shot!"

I shrug free, and stand my ground.

The Watcher smiles.

"You have proven your foolishness once again, Orb Master," he says. "One does not need sight to have vision. Just as one does not need great insight to understand we are all pawns in a game in which we have no control."

Game? What nonsense is he talking about? "Sure, big guy," I say, turning to the Zodiac. "Let's get out of here. This guy *is* nuts."

"You may leave if you wish," the Watcher says. "But if you do, you will not gain the knowledge you so desperately seek. As I have been so painfully reminded, I am not to interfere in the affairs of the universe. But, seeing how you have come such a long way, I will risk making an exception. You may ask me one question."

Scorpio raises a hand, stopping us. "Hold on." He turns to the Watcher. "What happened to Aries?"

The Watcher raises an eyebrow. "Is this the question

you most wish for me to answer? How about you, Orb Master? Is this *your* one burning question?"

I know the Zodiac wants to find out what happened to Aries, but I have something else I need to know.

Something all this 'Orb Master' talk is making me think about.

Something I've been suspecting for a long time.

I approach the Watcher and swallow hard. "Is the Orb of Oblivion still out there?" I ask. "Did it survive?"

The Watcher smirks. "As you have said yourself, the Orb of Oblivion is an entity—a cosmic entity, but an entity nonetheless."

Wait, I didn't say that out loud. I thought it, but I didn't say it.

"And as all creatures are born with an innate biological tendency towards self-preservation, the Orb took whatever steps were necessary to ensure its own survival. Therefore, I am certain that if you are searching for the Orb of Oblivion, you will not have to travel far."

What does that mean? I won't have to travel—

And then it hits me.

The Orb of Oblivion is … inside of me!

Suddenly, I feel sick to my stomach.

I hear the Watcher's deep laughter echoing in my brain.

Then, everything gets blurry, and my knees buckle. Suddenly, I'm floating. I look up to find Taurus glancing down at me, my arms and legs bouncing up and down. Is she carrying me? Stars drift past overhead, and then fade to darkness.

**

I wake up strapped in a chair. There's a low humming noise, and I'm being gently bounced around. I open my eyes and take in my surroundings. We're back on the Ghost Ship. Members of the Zodiac are walking back and forth, checking controls and pushing buttons. I lean over and look out the window. We're deep in space. There's no sign of Watcher World.

I slide back in my chair, the realization of what the Watcher said still sinking in. This can't be happening. I thought I was done with the Orb. I mean, I watched the High Commander take it aboard his ship. I sensed it blowing up somewhere in the universe. But instead of being destroyed, the Orb somehow stuck to me.

It just doesn't make any sense.

I close my eyes, and breathe deep. Then, I reach into my mind to connect with the Orb, to talk to it like I was able to do before, but there's nothing.

Nothing at all.

My mind drifts back to my family. I wonder what they're thinking? My parents are probably panicked. I can just see TechnocRat working all night in his lab figuring out a way to track me down. I've been gone so long I'm sure even Grace is missing me. And Dog-Gone—well, hopefully that fur ball is okay. Boy, it'd be great to see him again.

But, I'm stuck here. All on my own.

Some hero I am.

First, I'm kicked off the Freedom Force because I can't control my powers. Now, I'm stuck in outer space with no shot of getting home.

I feel a tear slide down my cheek, and wipe it away quickly. *Never show weakness.*

I watch Leo swing over to Scorpio. They both look my way, and start whispering back and forth.

I'm sure they're talking about where to dump me.

Just then, Gemini slides into the seat next to me. "So, how are you feeling?"

"You mean, after learning I've got an alien parasite wedged in my body, or realizing I may never see my family again?"

Gemini antenna's droop, and she looks down. Ugh! I totally forgot about her situation. That was a really insensitive thing to say.

"Sorry," I say embarrassed. "I forgot your whole world is gone."

"It's okay," she says, rubbing her eyes. "I mean, I'm just getting used to the idea. Truthfully, I'm still in shock. Thankfully, I found the Zodiac—they're like my new family. A dysfunctional family, but a family nonetheless."

"Yeah, they seem like a good group. Except for Leo. He gives me the creeps."

"He's a little strange, but he means well," she says. "I have to say, you impressed me on Watcher World, I didn't expect you to take it to him like that." She flips a strand of hair off her face, and smiles at me kind of funny.

"Thanks," I say, feeling myself turning red. "Honestly, neither did I. But, he just got my goat. I mean, what's his deal anyway? I didn't expect him to be blind. I thought he was supposed to see everything?"

"I know," Gemini says. "The legends never said anything about that. And what did he mean when he said he was 'painfully reminded' about interfering in the affairs of the—"

"Scorpio!" Pisces yells from the helm. "We've got company!"

I lean over and look out the windshield. To my surprise there are several large ships surrounding us—ships I've seen before—Skelton warships!

"But how did they find us?" Scorpio says.

"We're being hailed!" Pisces says.

Suddenly, the image of a square-jawed, yellow skinned man appears on the screen. He wiggles his pointy ears as he scans our faces with his neon-green eyes. Then I realize he's wearing a crown on his head.

It's the freaking Skelton Emperor!

This is not good.

"I am not patient," he begins. "So, I will be direct. You are harboring a known intergalactic criminal and enemy of the Skelton Empire. This miscreant is responsible for aiding a known traitor in the unprovoked murder of a Blood Bringer platoon, as well as the destruction of an imperial Skelton warship. For your own freedom, I advise you to turn the offender over immediately or be implicated as an accomplice in his nefarious acts."

What? That's not what happened!

"Pardon me, just stating the obvious," Leo says to the team, "but that's the Skelton Emperor. We should really think this through."

What? I thought he was on my side?

But he's right, if the Zodiac have any chance of making it out alive, I'll need to give myself up. Otherwise, the Emperor will kill every last one of them. I look at Gemini. They've suffered too much. I can't let that happen.

Scorpio looks at me, and then turns to the Emperor. "I'm sorry," he starts. "But—"

"Wait!" I say, stepping forward. "I appreciate what you're about to do, but I'll go."

"What?" Gemini says. "You can't—"

"No," I say. "It's okay. Let me go, and then you guys should get out of here as fast as you can."

"But he'll kill you," Taurus says, her fists clenched.

"And if I don't go, he'll kill *you*," I say. "All of you. Trust me, this is for the best." I stride to the center of the bridge and face the Emperor. "Take me. I'm ready."

The Skelton Emperor can barely conceal his glee. "Beam over the Orb Master," he commands. "Now."

Orb Master? This isn't about my so-called 'crimes' at all, is it? He wants me because of the Orb!

Suddenly, I feel a strange sensation.

I look down to see a crackling orange energy around my arms. Suddenly, my feet leave the ground. I'm being lifted into the air!

This doesn't seem like any teleportation device?

"What is happening?" I hear the Emperor shout. "I ordered you morons to beam him across!"

Wait a minute! This is what happened to Siphon! And the Overlord!

"Elliott!" Gemini screams.

I see her racing towards me.

And then everything goes black.

Meta Profile

Name: Watcher
Role: Cosmic Entity   Status: Active

VITALS:

Race: Inapplicable
Real Name: Watcher
Height: 10'0"
Weight: Unknown
Eye Color: White
Hair Color: Bald

META POWERS:

Class: Inapplicable
Power Level: Incalculable

- Observes all events in the universe
- Cannot interfere in any way, or will suffer dire consequences

CHARACTERISTICS:

Combat	Inapplicable
Durability	Inapplicable
Leadership	Inapplicable
Strategy	Inapplicable
Willpower	Inapplicable

EIGHT

I ENTER A GAME OF NIGHTMARES

I'm in a bed.

But it's not my bed. The covers are stiff, and the pillow is too thin. I also don't feel the weight of Dog-Gone pressing against my body. Usually, he hogs the covers and pushes me to the edge. This time I'm all alone—and, for once, I don't think that's a good thing.

I don't know where I am, or how I got here. Then it all comes racing back to me, and my stomach drops in dread. The last thing I remember is being swept up in that mysterious, orange energy that zapped Syphon and the Overlord. On one hand, it saved me from being delivered to the Skelton Emperor's warship. But on the other, it may have killed me, so if I'm in heaven right now I'll be really, really annoyed.

I open my eyes, only to be blinded by bright lights glaring above. I shield my eyes, and take in my surroundings. Well, if I'm not dead, I'm guessing it's the next best thing.

I'm in a small, white room roughly the size of a minivan. Other than the bed I'm lying in, which is sitting smack dab in the middle of the room, the only piece of furniture is a white bench to my right where my costume is sitting—neatly folded. So, wait a minute, does that mean ...

I peek under the covers and realize I'm wearing white pajamas.

Whew!

That could have been embarrassing.

Hold on! I don't remember putting on pajamas!

Wonderful.

As my eyes adjust, I notice something else that's weird. There's no door. So, how in the world did I—

"Good morning," comes a voice.

I jump out of my skin.

To my right, sitting on the bench, is a tall, thin man who simply wasn't there a second ago. He has white, slicked back hair and pale, purplish skin. He's wearing a crisp, black business suit with a white pocket square and tie. What's even more bizarre is that his eyes don't have pupils—instead, they're filled with stars.

"My apologies, I did not intend to alarm you," he says, pulling out a small, round tin from inside his jacket.

"Mint? After sleeping for so many days, I can only imagine how foul your mouth must taste."

"Who are *you*?" I ask. "And exactly how long did you say I've been sleeping?"

"Suit yourself," the man says, opening the tin and popping a small, white mint in his mouth. "To answer your first question, I am known as Order. As for your second question, you have been slumbering for five days, four hours, twenty three minutes, and thirteen seconds. Exactly."

"What?" I say. "Are you serious?"

"You will find that I am always serious," Order says.

"Okay," I say. "Can I, um, go home now?"

"Home?" Order says. "Oh, I am afraid not. You have been chosen to participate in a most important contest."

"Contest? What contest?"

Order smiles, his teeth are perfectly straight. "I see you are confused," he says. "Do not worry, everything will be made clear in time. But first, I think it would be best to show you what you are playing for."

Order snaps, and an image of outer space appears on the wall. A black and pink planet hovers in the center, surrounded by three smaller moons.

"This is Protaraan," he says, cheerfully. "One of my favorite worlds. It has a truly marvelous landscape—with vast grasslands and deep, majestic seas. It is the home to some of the galaxy's most wondrous creatures. The

Protaraan people are industrious and peaceful, and the wildlife is plentiful and diverse. Did you know there are ten thousand four hundred and ninety three sub-species of crustaceans alone?"

Suddenly, a tiny speck appears, like a firefly in the night, heading straight for Protaraan. As it advances, it leaves a bright trail behind it, like the tail of a comet.

The image pushes in closer, and I realize that firefly is actually a person. A man—made of fire!

"Who's that?" I ask.

"The Herald," Order sighs, "signaling the beginning of the end."

I have no clue what he means by that. I watch as this Herald dude starts circling Protaraan over and over again, his trail getting brighter and brighter, until a shape emerges resembling electrons encircling the nucleus of an atom—which, in this case, is Protaraan. In my gut, I feel like something bad is about to happen, and I'm not sure I want to stick around to find out what.

"Well, what do you know?" I say, turning to Order. "That Herald certainly puts on quite a show. So, what's next? We go for milkshakes and call it a night?"

But Order doesn't respond. He's fixated on the events unfolding before us. Reluctantly, I turn back to the image and do a double take.

Creeping in from the bottom of the scene is a mysterious, green mist. At first, it's narrow and stringy, but as it approaches Protaraan it expands larger and larger until it covers the surface area of the entire planet itself! The Herald bolts from the scene, leaving a fiery trail behind him.

Now I can't even see Protaraan through the green haze. I'm about to ask Order what's going on, when the green cloud suddenly solidifies—and then clamps down on the planet's surface!

That green thing is ... alive?

The green mass pulsates, and then, without warning, it constricts, applying an incredible amount of pressure to the trapped world. There's a tremendous CRACKING sound.

"It's crushing it!"

"No," Order says. "It is consuming it."

KABOOM!

Suddenly, there's a deafening explosion accompanied by a blinding flash of light! I shield my eyes, but I'm not quick enough. For a few seconds, all I can see is white. My ears are ringing like crazy. When I'm finally able to blink my way back to vision, my jaw drops.

Protaraan is gone.

All that remains is a sea of pebbles floating aimlessly in space. At the top of the image I catch the tail of a green mist, moving slowly out of frame.

"I-It's gone!" I say astonished. "All of those people are ... are ..."

"Extinct," Order says. "Now you understand the magnitude of what you will be playing for—the fate of an entire planet."

"I-I don't understand?" I say.

And then it clicks.

That green mist that ate Protaraan is …

"Ravager!" I blurt out.

"Yes," Order says. "Ravager. The Annihilator of Worlds."

That freaky thing destroyed the homes or Gemini, Scorpio, and the rest of the Zodiac! That's the cosmic creature the Orb of Oblivion was supposed to destroy? How the heck am I supposed to stop that?

My mind is racing. I still have no clue what I'm doing here. Or, more importantly, how I'm going to get out of here. I breathe deeply, and try to re-center myself. If I don't figure this out I've got no chance of getting home.

"Okay," I say. "Let's cut to the chase. How do I play this game you're talking about. And how am I gonna get back home?"

"It is quite simple," Order says, dabbing his eyes with his white handkerchief. "You have been selected as a galactic champion—my champion—to compete for the fate of a planet. If you win, the planet survives. But if you lose …"

"It's eaten by Ravager?" I finish his sentence.

"Yes," Order says, standing. He clasps his hands behind his back, and begins pacing. "It has been this way through all of eternity. You see, my brother, Chaos, and I are tasked with keeping all things in proper balance. My job is to ensure structure, discipline, and boundaries. My brother's role is quite the opposite. His job is to promote stress, disorder, and randomness. We are constantly at odds. To be truthful, I find it all quite exhausting."

"So, you're like … Gods or something?" I ask.

"Oh, no," Order says. "We are more than Gods. Much more. You could say we are the very fabric of the universe."

"That does sound exhausting," I acknowledge.

"Indeed" he says. "Instead of constantly trying to undo all the other has done, we have agreed to a simple contest to be held after the birth of a new solar system. What I just shared with you was a replay of the outcome of our last contest. Unfortunately, my champions lost. That is where I hope you will come in."

"What do I need to do?" I ask.

"You, and three other champions I have selected, will compete to recover a hidden artifact. The team that recovers the artifact first will determine the fate of a planet. If my team wins, the planet will survive for another million years. If my brother's team wins, the planet will be sacrificed to Ravager, and his champions will be granted new worlds to rule."

He stares at me as I process what he said.

This isn't a game of tiddlywinks he's talking about here. I mean, I don't even have control over my powers. Doesn't he want to win? Maybe he should have picked Dad or Mom or anyone else on the Freedom Force. But not me!

"Hey, listen," I say. "I'm really flattered you want me on your team. I mean, I'm never picked first for anything, not even checkers. But this is serious stuff you're talking about. I think you've got the wrong guy."

Order smiles again. "I have observed millions of champions in my time. Sometimes I am right. Sometimes I am wrong. But, you have been selected, and therefore, you must compete."

"And what if I refuse?"

"As our agreement stipulates, if any selected champion refuses to participate, then that team must automatically forfeit the match. And, if that team is mine, an entire planet will be destroyed."

I breathe deeply. I think about Gemini and what's happened to her world. She's lost everything she's ever known. I could never willingly let that happen to anyone else. I couldn't imagine being responsible for the deaths of billions of people.

"You've got me there," I say. "Okay, I guess I'm in."

"As I knew you would be," Order says. "Now please, get some rest, and eat." He snaps again, and a tray of food appears at the foot of the bed. There's pizza, and cucumbers, and tortilla chips, and root beer. All of my favorite things! It smells amazing!

I dive in. It feels like I haven't eaten for days.

"Tomorrow, you will meet your teammates," Order says. "But before I leave you, I will share with you what you will be playing for in *your* contest."

He snaps again, but I'm so famished all I can focus on is the food.

"When the door appears tomorrow morning," Order says, "make sure you exit wearing your costume."

At this point, I'm totally pigging out. I should probably ask what I'm supposed to do when I need to use the bathroom, but when I look up, Order is gone.

I glance over to see what it is I'll supposedly be playing for. And that's when I drop my pizza.

Because hovering before me is a familiar blue-green planet.

Earth.

Meta Profile

Name: Order
Role: Cosmic Entity   Status: Active

VITALS:

Race: Inapplicable
Real Name: Order
Height: appears 7'0"
Weight: Unknown
Eye Color: Inapplicable
Hair Color: White

META POWERS:

Class: Inapplicable
Power Level: Incalculable

- Balances his brother, Chaos, to ensure structure, discipline, and boundaries throughout the universe
- Cannot harm other Cosmic Entities

CHARACTERISTICS:

Combat	Inapplicable
Durability	Inapplicable
Leadership	Inapplicable
Strategy	Inapplicable
Willpower	Inapplicable

NINE

I GET MISTAKEN FOR SOMEBODY ELSE

Needless to say, I didn't sleep a wink.

I mean, how could I after learning my actions will determine the fate of Earth! I tossed and turned all night long, thinking about all of those innocent people down there, and all those kids just going about their business worrying about pimples, homework, and social media cred. They have no clue what's going on up here. None of them are fighting for their lives to stop a globe-gobbling pile of glop!

Nope. Apparently, only I'm dumb enough to get signed up for that one.

And what the heck *am* I doing here anyway? Why would Order pick me? I mean, I'm just a kid, not some freaking galactic gladiator. Why didn't he choose Dad, or Mom, or even Grace? They're playing in the big leagues with full control of their powers. Me? I'm squarely in the minors with no clue how my powers work.

I look around the tiny room. There's no clock so I have no idea what time it is. Order said a door would magically appear when he's ready for me—whenever the heck that is.

To my surprise, a door did appear at one point. Thinking it was game-time, I got suited up, only to burst through the door and crash into a toilet. So, instead of answering the call of adventure, I answered the call of nature.

Yep, villains fear me.

It feels like I've spent hours in solitary confinement. To prevent myself from going stir crazy, I've done everything from jumping jacks to the Hokey Pokey. But mostly, I've done a lot of thinking.

Especially about the Orb of Oblivion.

What I don't get is if the Orb is somehow inside of me, then why isn't it working like it did before? The last time I had it, we were mind-linked, and it was talking to me like crazy. Now there's complete radio silence. I'm beginning to suspect it's mad at me for blowing it up, which is probably justified.

The Orb is a cosmic parasite. When it was a physical entity, outside my body, it mentally bonded to its host and fed off their deepest desires. So, what's it doing now that it's inside of me? The image of a radioactive tapeworm comes to mind.

I'm feeling totally restless, so I hop off the bed to top my astounding push-up record of five when I notice something unusual.

There's a door.

A gold door.

The last door that materialized was white. So, I'm guessing this has to be the one!

I rush over to put on my costume when, suddenly, I get the jitters. Is this really it? If so, what happens next could determine the fate of everyone on Earth— including my family.

And it's all up to me.

I pull on my mask, and straighten my cape. The words of a brave friend echo in my mind: *Never show weakness.*

I take a deep breath, and push through the door.

I step into a large, white chamber with walls that climb hundreds of feet high. There are gold doors all around the perimeter, just like the one I entered from. The chamber is windowless, so I still can't tell whether its day or night.

Order mentioned I'd be meeting my teammates, but there's nobody here but—

"Are you friend, or foe?" comes a voice.

I spin around to find a stern-faced man standing behind me. Where'd he come from? His dark eyes study me from beneath a thick, leather headband adorned with the symbol of a black eagle. With his long, black hair, and tan costume he appears Native American, but his skin is blue! He folds his arms across his broad chest and repeats, "Friend, or foe?"

"Friend," I say quickly. "I-I think we're supposed to be teammates."

The man studies me, and then extends a hand. "I am called Wind Walker, Crosser of Realms."

I shake his hand. "And I'm Epic Zero, a member of the Freedom Force. Well, sometimes I'm a member of the Freedom Force. I mean, when I'm not grounded." I smile lamely.

I can tell by his arched eyebrows he's far from impressed. Way to go, Elliott.

Suddenly, another door opens, and a large figure emerges. At first I think it's a man, but he looks young—like he's only a few years older than me. His muscles are huge, but that's not his most impressive feature. That belongs to the pair of long, curved horns protruding from his forehead. Could it be?

"Please," he says, squeezing his giant hands into fists, "tell me you're the bad guys, because I want to get this over with, and get back to my friends."

"Whoa, big fella," I say. "You're Aries, aren't you?"

He looks at me funny, trying to place me. "How'd you know that? Who are you?"

"My name is Epic Zero," I say, trying to muster

more confidence this time around. "I'm a hero on my world, a member of the Freedom Force. For the last few days, I've been travelling with your team, the Zodiac."

There, that was better.

He looks me up and down. "You're Epic Zero? You're kidding me?"

Or not.

Suddenly, there's a SLAM.

"What's he doing here?" comes an angry, female voice.

I turn to find a girl standing in the doorway. She has long brown hair, and wears a blue mask and bodysuit with white shooting stars across her top and legs. Wait, why do I know that costume? And how come her angry expression look so familiar?

Then, she points at me, and commands. "Stand down, super-creep!"

Wait? What? Super-creep? Me? Her voice is so familiar.

"Who are you?" Aries asks.

"Who am I?" she says. "I'm Glory Girl. And I'm taking this goober out."

Glory Girl? Grace?

But Grace doesn't have brown hair?

The next thing I know, she charges me. But before she gets far, she's frozen in her tracks.

"Halt, heroes!"

I try turning, but I'm frozen too!

Just then, Order appears, hovering in the air above us. He lands without a sound, and snaps his fingers. Suddenly, we can move again.

"I suggest you refrain from harming one another," Order says. "After all, you will soon be working together."

"Are you nuts?" Grace exclaims. "I'm not working with him! He took over my entire planet!"

"Grace, what are you talking about?" I ask, totally confused.

"Don't you dare call me by my first name, you tyrant!" she screams back.

"What?" I say. "What's wrong with you?"

"There is nothing wrong with her," Order says. "For, on her world, you *are* a tyrant."

"Her world? What are you talking about?" I say, more confused than ever.

"Perhaps I can explain," Wind Walker says. "For my powers allow me to walk between worlds—and between universes."

"Hold on there," I say. "Are you saying there's more than one universe?"

"Yes," Wind Walker says. "I am certain that you perceive your reality—the here and now—as the only form of reality—as a single, unfolding series of events. But the truth of reality is far more complex. For while we are standing here in our universe, there are other realities co-existing to ours—mirror universes, in a sense—where events still unfold in a chronological manner, but with drastically different outcomes."

"So you're saying there are two of her?" I say, pointing to Grace. The very thought makes me shiver.

Wind Walker smiles. "Yes, just as there may be hundreds of mirror worlds, there may be hundred of versions of her, just as there may be hundreds of versions of you."

"Hundreds of Graces," I say. "I think you just exploded my brain." If he's serious than that would explain why she has brown hair instead of blond. And why her costume is blue instead of crimson. That's not my sister! It's some freaky alternate universe version of my sister!

"So, hang on," I say. "You mean, on your world I'm like, the king?"

Grace folds her arms and spits. "I didn't say king. I said tyrant."

"Cool!" I say.

"Enough," Order says. "There is little time, and you must learn the rules."

Grace shoots me a nasty look. I wouldn't trade my sister for this version any day of the week.

Order snaps, and a holographic map segmented by gridlines appears. "You will be battling on Arena World—a planet with varied terrain and extreme weather conditions. Do not underestimate these facts. How you deal with Arena World may ultimately contribute to your victory, or your defeat."

Well, that sounds ominous.

"As I have explained to each of you," Order continues, "you will be competing against the team of my brother, Chaos, to recover a hidden artifact. This is the artifact you seek." Order snaps, and a silver cube with an orange glow materializes. "This is the Building Block. I must warn you, the Building Block is not just an object— it is a sentient being. Therefore, you may want to consider it as a player in its own right. And it can be deadly."

Great, now we've got to fetch a tissue box with attitude problems.

Order snaps again and the image of Arena World shifts to an image of Earth. "This is a battle with the ultimate stakes. If you are defeated, billions will lose their lives. Today, you will get to know one another and learn how to work together. You will practice as a team, and become familiar with each other's powers."

I peer over at Grace, who's still giving me the evil eye.

"And tomorrow," Order continues, "you will fight for your lives. But, before I depart, I think it is only fair to reveal who you will be facing in combat. Study my brother's team carefully, and determine your course to victory."

He snaps again, and disappears, leaving behind four holographic images of our enemies.

There's some villain I don't know, but is a deadringer for a Skelton Blood Bringer.

And then, there's Siphon!

The Overlord!

And ... Mom?

Meta Profile

Name: Glory Girl (2)
Role: Hero   Status: Active

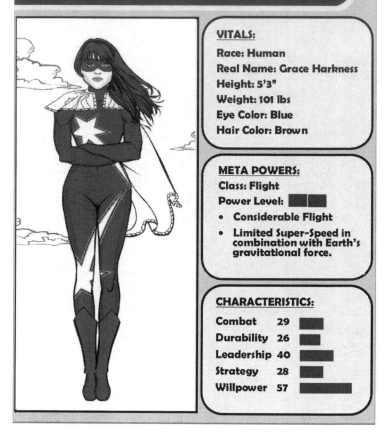

VITALS:

Race: Human
Real Name: Grace Harkness
Height: 5'3"
Weight: 101 lbs
Eye Color: Blue
Hair Color: Brown

META POWERS:

Class: Flight
Power Level:
- Considerable Flight
- Limited Super-Speed in combination with Earth's gravitational force.

CHARACTERISTICS:

Combat   29
Durability 26
Leadership 40
Strategy   28
Willpower   57

TEN

I COMPLETELY HUMILIATE MYSELF

So much for working as a team.

After Order dropped the bomb about our competitors, he vanished without a trace. Then, instead of coming together as a team to strategize, the four of us wandered into separate corners. Truthfully, that's fine by me, because after what's transpired in the last five minutes, there's a heck of a lot I need to process.

First, I still need to wrap my head around this mirror universe thing. It's hard to imagine there's some duplicate of me out there doing things I couldn't even dream of— like, for example, conquering Earth. I mean, how'd something like that even happen? I can't believe it's even real.

But, then again, it's impossible to write off when a

duplicate of my sister is pacing back and forth less than twenty feet away. To keep everything straight in my mind, I've labeled her Grace 2—and it's pretty clear she hates me. I really don't know how we're ever going to work together to save Earth.

And then there's the other doozy.

Apparently, we're going to be fighting Mom!

I mean, clearly she's not my mom—my mom's a hero through and through. So, that means on some bizarre Earth, Mom is a villain! This is like, total insanity! I don't know if this version of mom is from the same Earth as Grace 2 or not. I guess she could be Mom 2, Mom 3, or Mom 103 for all I know.

My head is pounding.

Before Order split, he left behind a buffet with all sorts of food on it. I see Wind Walker and Aries loading up their plates and talking. My stomach is rumbling, so I figure I'd better grab something now. After all, who knows how long it'll be until I can eat again.

As I approach, I catch the heroes in mid-conversation.

"—don't know if they can work together," Wind Walker says.

"Fabulous," Aries says. "Then we're as good as dead."

"How's it going, fellas?" I say, grabbing a chicken drumstick.

Aries looks at me with a serious expression. "If we're

going to have any chance at winning this thing, you're going to have to bury the hatchet with her."

"Me?" I say. "You saw what happened. She's got the problem, remember?"

We look over at Grace 2, who's now sitting with her back against the wall, her head resting on her knees.

"That may be true," Wind Walker says. "But it is up to you to solve it. The lives of billions depend on it."

"Why is it my job? She started it! I didn't do anything to offend her, but breathe."

I glance back over to see her wiping away a tear.

Suddenly, my dad's words pop into my head. *"We're heroes,"* Dad said. *"We're sworn to help all of those in need."*

Sometimes it stinks being the good guy.

"Fine," I say, looking at Wind Walker and Aries. "I'll do it."

But how? Out of the corner of my eye, I spy a pile of jelly doughnuts on the table. Maybe ...

I grab a napkin, wrap up a doughnut, and take a deep breath. Then I walk over to Grace 2 and slide down next to her.

"Jelly doughnut?" I offer. "They're my sister's favorite."

"Thanks," Grace 2 says, "mine, too." She reaches for the doughnut and takes a big bite. "Sorry for attacking you," she says, talking with her mouth full. "I lost my marbles when I thought you were someone else. But I guess you're you, and not the person I thought you were."

"No problem," I say. "You really caught me off guard. I mean, I didn't know about this whole mirror universe thing. It kind of blows my mind when I think about it."

"Yeah, me too," Grace 2 says. "It's weird."

I study her closely as she chews. Except for her brown hair, she's the spitting image of my sister, even down to the freckles on her nose.

Unbelievable.

"So," I say, "if you don't mind me asking. Was that your mom up there? I mean, mine's a hero on my world."

Grace 2 breathes out. "Yeah, that's my mom—Ms. Understood. I haven't seen her since she and my dad got divorced."

"Divorced?" I exclaim.

"Yeah," Grace 2 continues. "She used to be a superhero, but then turned into a villain. My dad was pretty bummed about it, so much so that he actually hung up his tights. Especially after—well, after you became supreme ruler and outlawed all superheroes."

"I did what?"

"Outlawed all heroes," Grace 2 repeats. "You offered a bounty to anyone that brought you a superhero. And once you got them, you cancelled their powers— permanently. It then became a free-for-all for the villains, who pretty much did whatever they wanted. They started forming these Meta gangs, marking their turf. But there's still an underground group of heroes like me that work day and night to stop you. We call ourselves the Freedom Force. And one day, we're going to take you down and set the world right again."

I watch her get more and more agitated as she speaks.

"Hang on," I say. "Remember, it's not me who's doing this. It's your brother on *your* world."

"Sorry," she says, deflating. "You're right. This whole thing is so overwhelming. And then to see my mom up there ..."

"Hey," I say, putting my hand on her shoulder. "I get it. But we're the heroes, right? We need to save the day when others won't."

She smiles at me, "You're right. I guess if we're going to work together, we should put this behind us, shouldn't we?"

She reaches out her hand, and we shake.

"By the way, Elliott," she adds, "you're blond in my universe."

"What?" I say. "You're kidding?"

As we stand up, we're joined by Wind Walker and Aries. Aries gives me a nod. "We good?" he asks.

"Yeah," I say. "We're good."

"Excellent," says Wind Walker. "Now we must learn about each other's powers and abilities."

"And that is precisely why I have returned," comes Order's voice from above, spooking the pants off of us.

"I'm getting tired of this guy," Grace 2 whispers.

"Prepare yourselves," Order says.

Suddenly, all of the gold doors around the chamber pop open.

"I don't have a good feeling about this," Aries says.

"This exercise will not be as difficult as the task you will face tomorrow," Order says. "Nonetheless, it should prove quite ... educational." And with that, he disappears.

"Close ranks," Wind Walker says, and we all gather back-to-back in the center of the room, awaiting the arrival of whatever nightmare Order is about to throw at us.

We stand there for what feels like an eternity. I take a deep breath. These guys are counting on me to pull my weight, but I can't even control my powers. I need to make sure that when I use them, I don't accidentally cancel out theirs.

That is, as long as whatever it is we're about to face even has Meta powers. Because if it's anything else, then I'm essentially useless.

Just then, we hear beeping—lots of loud, high-pitched beeping. Like there's some big hullabaloo among a bunch of—

"Robots!" Grace 2 yells.

Robots. Of course, robots.

I'm about to inform my teammates that I'll be as useful as a pinecone, when the mechanical monsters are on top of us. They're big and fast. I barely catch their features—menacing red eyes, pincer-like arms, and spiked, spinning wheels—as they head straight for us.

I dive out of the way in the nick of time, as a bot slides past me, leaving behind a giant skid mark.

This isn't good! My powers don't work on robots!

But, apparently, they're no problem for my teammates.

Aries holds his ground, shattering robot after robot with his powerful fists! Wind Walker's opened some kind of mystical void around his body that's like a roach motel—robots check in, but they don't check out! And Grace 2 has taken to the air, picking up robots one by one, and dropping them to their doom from terrifying heights!

We'd probably get out of this mess if it wasn't for the fact that the robots just keep coming—wave after automated wave.

I'm pretty much dead meat sitting here, so I pick myself up and bolt towards Wind Walker. Maybe he can protect both of us with that rift thing he's got going on. I make it halfway when I suddenly realize my feet aren't touching the ground anymore.

I'm floating! With a robot latched onto each arm!

I try to pull free, but their grip is too strong.

"Help!" I call, but the other heroes have their hands full.

We're cruising at a good clip when the robots

suddenly change course. Before us is a giant column in the corner of the chamber—a thick, marble column.

"Put me down!" I yell.

But they don't listen. Instead, they make a bee-line straight for it, which can only mean one thing.

They're going to smash me against it!

We pick up speed!

We're going so fast I can't even speak, my face is stretched back like I'm nose-diving in an airplane. The column is getting closer and closer. We're going to crash!

I close my eyes.

And one overriding thought takes over.

STOP!

Suddenly, there's a deafening SCREECH, and I'm jerked forwards. The robots release their grip, and I go flying head over heels, landing inches away from the base of the column.

What happened?

I turn, to find the two robots standing stock-still behind me—stopped dead in their tracks.

I thought it ...

... and they did it?

But that's not my power? My powers only work on Metas. I-I haven't been able to do that since ... since ...

O.

M.

G.

"Epic!" Grace 2 calls from above. "Are you okay?

Sorry I couldn't get here faster."

"Yeah," I say, standing up. "I'm good."

"Nice work," she says, landing beside me. "Funny, your powers are exactly the same as my brother's."

"Really?" I say. For some reason, that gives me a weird feeling, but I can't put my finger on why. I'm just so confused right now.

Seconds later, we're joined by Aries and Wind Walker. There's a mountain of robot parts behind them.

"Everyone okay?" Aries asks.

"Yep," Grace 2 says. "We're fine. I guess we showed those tin-bots a thing or two."

"Indeed," Wind Walker says. "But we fought as individuals. If we are going to be victorious tomorrow, we will need to fight as a team."

"I agree," Aries says. "Otherwise, we'll have no chance. I'm pretty clear on your powers," he says looking at Wind Walker and Grace 2. "But what exactly do you do?" he says, looking at me.

"Me?" I say, stalling for time. "Great question." What do I tell him? My Meta Manipulation powers can cancel the powers of other Metas. But that doesn't explain what I just did to those robots who don't have powers.

"He's omnipotent," Grace 2 says. "Just like my brother on my world."

Omnipo-what?

"Omnipotent?" Aries says. "What's that mean?"

"It means all powerful," Grace 2 says. "If he thinks it, it'll happen. Isn't that right, Epic?"

All powerful? Wait a minute. Is that what the Orb of Oblivion is—omnipotent? And it's … inside of me.

"Epic?" Grace 2 repeats.

I look up to find them staring at me. "Yeah," I say. "That's right."

"Well, then" Aries says, breaking into a huge smile. "Now I see why Leo wanted you. I guess we don't have anything to worry about." He puts his big hand on my shoulder. "We've got Epic Zero."

"Right," I say, faking a smile. "I guess we do."

Meta Profile

Name: Aries
Role: Vigilante   Status: Active

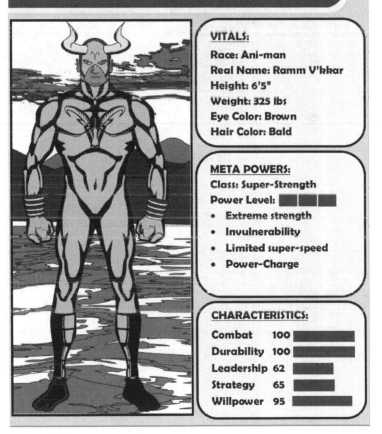

VITALS:

Race: Ani-man
Real Name: Ramm V'kkar
Height: 6'5"
Weight: 325 lbs
Eye Color: Brown
Hair Color: Bald

META POWERS:

Class: Super-Strength
Power Level: ▮▮▮
- Extreme strength
- Invulnerability
- Limited super-speed
- Power-Charge

CHARACTERISTICS:

Combat	100
Durability	100
Leadership	62
Strategy	65
Willpower	95

ELEVEN

I GO OUT OF MY MIND

Let's just say Order was less than impressed.

He muttered something about picking the wrong group of heroes, and then sent us back to our rooms to rest up for tomorrow's battle to the death. That's okay by me because, honestly, I'm still not sure what happened out there.

It's no secret I was in serious danger with those robots out there. I mean, I thought I was going to croak! But, instead, the Orb of Oblivion took over.

Believe me, I'm grateful to be alive. But, I'm also freaking terrified.

Especially after hearing what Grace 2 had to say. Because if she thinks her brother's powers are like mine, then I'm going to have a bigger fight on my hands then finding the Building Block. After all, her brother is pure evil.

Of course, he and I aren't the same person. I mean, I suppose it's possible that I'm just a good guy and he's a natural psychopath. A good example of that is Mom—she's a hero on my world, but a villain on Grace 2's world. But there's also another possibility.

One that's less pleasant to think about.

Maybe he *was* good just like me, but then *turned* evil. Not because he wanted to be a villain, but because he couldn't help it—because he was corrupted—by a second Orb of Oblivion.

The thought sends a chill down my spine.

Two Orbs of Oblivion?

It's staggering to even consider it. But the more I think about it, the more I realize it must be true.

How else could he have become king? I mean, my powers are strong, but not that strong! And how else could he permanently cancel a Meta's powers? Grace 2's words echo in my mind: *If he thinks it, it'll happen.*

Isn't that how the Orb works?

So, if that's also true for him …

I think back to what happened with those robots, and remember the Watcher's words: *the Orb took whatever steps were necessary to ensure its own survival.* It's pretty clear. The Orb wouldn't let me die because it wanted to save itself!

And then I realize what's really happening. The Orb

is using me—resting inside of me—gathering its strength. And when it's ready, it's going to make its move.

Sweat drips down my forehead.

I mastered it before, but what if it's too strong this time? What if it turns me into a monster? What if it takes over my mind, and I become a puppet—a shell of a person—existing only to do its bidding?

It's only a matter of time.

I feel like puking.

Suddenly, I'm absolutely exhausted. My eyes start drooping, and my limbs feel like lead—like I'm sinking into the bed. I know I need sleep, but I have way too much to figure out. I try to fight it, but I'm slipping—going down. What's happening? Is this one of Order's tricks?

I need to stay awake.

I … need … to …

***

I'm sitting in a room under a blinding spotlight. I shield my eyes, when I notice the outline of someone sitting across from me—deep in the shadows.

"Why are you fighting it," comes a boy's voice. It sounds somehow familiar.

"What?" I say. "Who are you?"

"Why fight it?" he repeats. *"You know you want to be just like him."*

"Like who?" I say. "What are you talking about?"

The boy laughs. *"C'mon,"* he says. *"Do I need to spell it out for you? Like Elliott 2—Elliott the king—the most powerful Meta on his planet."*

"I don't want to be like him," I say.

"Don't you?" the boy says. *"Isn't it what you've always dreamed of? No one would be more powerful than you. You can make up all the rules—do whatever you want. You could make the world peaceful, or even rule it if you wanted. Who'd stop you?"*

"Who are you?" I ask. But, deep inside, I already know the answer.

"Let's not play games," he says. *"You need me. So, let me help you. I promise you won't regret it. You'll be thanking me later."*

"I don't want anything to do with you," I say. "I want you out. Tell me how to get you out."

"You know I can't do that," he says. *"I know you don't want to hear this, but you're the one. We're a team—a partnership to the end. Soon, you'll see. We're meant to be together."*

"Liar!" I yell, standing up from the chair.

The boy laughs. *"You'll see,"* he says. *"You'll see soon enough."*

"Get out!" I yell. "Get out of—"

***

"—me!"

I shoot up. I'm still in bed.

But I'm not alone.

"It is time," Order says, seated on the bench.

"I-it's morning already?" I ask. "I feel like I haven't slept at all."

"You slept," he says. "And dreamt."

I run my fingers through my hair. "I guess I did. I just don't know what it means."

"Do you know why I selected you?" Order asks.

"Because you want to see a world die?" I say.

"No, Elliott Harkness," he says, staring at me, the stars in his eyes twinkling bright. "Because I want to win. Not just for today, not just for tomorrow, but for all of eternity."

"O-okay?" I say. What's he's getting at?

He stands up, and folds his arms. "Can you imagine a universe where everything flourishes? Where there is no death, no destruction—where everything moves in perfectly predictable harmony, forever more."

For a second, I'm not following him. And then a lightbulb goes off.

"Wait a minute," I say. "Are you saying you want to get rid of Chaos? Like, lock him up or something."

"No," he says, looking down at me. "I want to destroy him."

What? Destroy Chaos? How do you destroy Chaos?

"B-but," I stammer, "wouldn't that throw everything, like, completely off balance. Don't you need him to keep the universe stable? I mean, don't we all kind of need him?"

Order's eyebrows furrow. "Do we? Did you enjoy watching Protaraan being destroyed? Did you hear the screams of a trillion creatures meeting their end? Do you think you will be able to save your planet? And even if you do, will your descendants be able to do the same when their time inevitably comes?

There's logic to what he's saying. But something just doesn't seem right.

"I I thought we were trying to stop Ravager?" I say. "I thought that's what this whole thing's about."

"That is what it has been about for millennia," he says. "But this time it will be different. Because I found you."

"Me? Why me?" I ask, although I'm pretty sure I'm not going to like the answer.

"While I possess great power," he says, "I am also constrained by it. I have limitations. For example, I am unable to harm another cosmic being. It is written in the stars."

"So ... what does that have to do with me?"

"You are the Orb Master," he says. "You are not a cosmic entity, yet you have a cosmic power growing inside of you. Thus, you are not constrained."

The words take a minute to sink in.

"Wait," I say, "so you're saying you want *me* to use the Orb of Oblivion to take down Chaos?"

Order smiles, his perfect teeth gleaming. "When the

appropriate moment arises, you will act."

"Are you kidding me?" I say, "I won't do it!"

"Oh, Orb Master, you will," he says. "You will because you will have no other choice."

I'm speechless. I ... I don't even know what to say.

"Now rise, and prepare yourself for battle," he says. "Put on your costume and join your teammates in the main chamber. The contest will start momentarily."

And then he snaps, and he's gone.

I grab my stomach.

I need to get this stinking Orb out of my body.

Before it's too late.

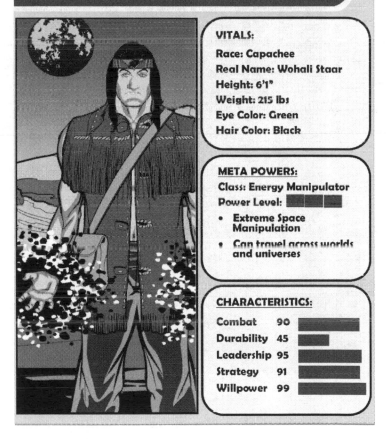

Meta Profile

Name: Wind Walker
Role: Hero   Status: Active

VITALS:

Race: Capachee
Real Name: Wohali Staar
Height: 6'1"
Weight: 215 lbs
Eye Color: Green
Hair Color: Black

META POWERS:

Class: Energy Manipulator
Power Level:
- **Extreme Space Manipulation**
- **Can travel across worlds and universes**

CHARACTERISTICS:

Combat   90
Durability 45
Leadership 95
Strategy   91
Willpower   99

TWELVE

I GET A BAD CASE OF DEJA VU

To say my head isn't in the game is an understatement.

Here we are, about to launch into the greatest battle in the history of mankind, and I can't stop thinking about what Order said: *"When the appropriate moment arises, you will act."*

What the heck does that mean?

Is he going to brainwash me into destroying Chaos? And, how exactly does one destroy Chaos anyway? I have a sneaking suspicion I'm going to find out, like it or not.

I consider mentioning my secret mission to my teammates, but decide against it. With so much at stake, I don't want anything distracting them from the task at hand. I mean, we have a whole planet to save! A planet with billions of people on it who are counting on us.

Including my family.

Looking at Grace 2, I can't help but think of them. The fact that I'll probably never see them again brings a tear to my eye, but I wipe it away. I need to be brave—that's what my parents would want. I suddenly have an overwhelming urge to wrap my arms around Dog-Gone, and nuzzle into his furry face. But I'll never get that chance again either.

I wonder if there's a Dog-Gone 2?

We're standing in the main chamber, waiting for Order to magically appear. Aries is jumping up and down, psyching himself up. Wind Walker is meditating peacefully in the corner. Grace 2 and I are just standing around, waiting for this nightmare to begin.

"You ready to go?" Grace 2 asks.

"As ready as I'm ever gonna be," I answer.

"You know," Grace 2 says. "It didn't really occur to me before, but whose Earth are we trying to save anyway?"

That's a great question! It hadn't dawned on me that maybe the Earth we're fighting for isn't mine. Maybe it's hers, or some other version. "Yeah, I hadn't thought of that either."

Suddenly, I have a sliver of hope. Maybe my family will be spared after all! Then again, knowing my luck, what are the odds of that? But I guess I wouldn't try any less if wasn't my Earth anyway. When lives are at stake, heroes don't mail it in.

"It doesn't matter," she says, "because we're gonna win anyway. Right?"

"Yeah," I say. "Right."

I'd love to be as optimistic as she is, but, truthfully, I'm not so sure.

Our briefing on our opponents was like a "Who's Who" of the galaxy's most dangerous Meta 3 villains: there's the Overlord, an Energy Manipulator who can control gravity; Siphon, a Meta Manipulator who can absorb the powers of others; some Skelton Meta-Morph shape-shifter who I'm sure will be a load-and-a-half; and, maybe the scariest of them all, Mom 2—a Psychic.

So, this isn't going to be a walk in the park.

Not by a long shot.

Just then, Order appears with the artifact—the Building Block—in his hands.

"Champions," he begins. "The time has come. Once again, take note of the object you seek—the Building Block. It will be hidden somewhere on Arena World. As I have warned, some of you may not survive this ordeal, but I urge you to always remember what you are fighting for." He snaps, and a hologram of Earth appears next to him.

I study it closely. It sure looks like my Earth. All the continents are the same. The oceans look about right. I just can't tell.

"I will remind you of the rules one final time," Order says. "If you recover the artifact first, you will preserve the lives of this world for another million years. If my brother, Chaos' team wins, the planet will be destroyed, and his champions will each be given a new planet to rule. Aside from this, there are no other rules. Now it is time to go forth and compete." He looks me in the eyes. "And to win."

Order snaps again, and we are suddenly encased in that strange orange energy that brought us all here in the first place.

I catch Grace 2's face, her eyes are wide.

I turn back to Order, who's smiling at me.

And then, he's gone.

***

We materialize in a valley encircled by sweeping, ice-capped mountains. As we touch down, our feet sink ankle-deep into the snow-covered ground. It's bitterly cold, and a sharp wind is whipping snowflakes sideways like sheets of rain.

It's a blizzard. Great.

Order was right when he said the terrain will be a big factor. Within seconds, I feel like a popsicle, Grace wraps herself in her cape, shivering like crazy, Wind Walker grits his teeth, and Aries' horns start collecting icicles.

If we don't get out of here fast, I don't think we'll make it to find the cube. But which way should we go? We're surrounded by giant, craggy mountains.

As if reading my mind, Grace 2 chatters, "A-allow m-me." Then she takes off into the air.

We watch her push upwards through the blustery sky, climbing higher and higher until we completely lose sight of her in the swirling wintery mix. She's gone for a long time. Soon, Wind Walker and Aries start looking as worried as I feel. I'm about to suggest we somehow go after her, when she suddenly drops back in our midst.

"What took you so long?" I ask.

"You're not going to believe it," she says, "but, that way," she points to the mountains in front of her, "is a city—like, a big honking city with buildings and streets and everything. And it's raining!." She turns the other direction, "and over there is a forest with trees, and vines, and it's bright and sunny."

Wow! This world *is* crazy.

"Well, I can't imagine the Building Block is buried here," Aries says, shuddering. "We'd die of hypothermia before we even found it. I say we hit those other areas."

"I agree," Wind Walker says. "And if we split up, we can cover more ground."

Grace 2 and I exchange looks. Even though we barely know each other, there's a familiarity between us that feels comforting. She nods.

"Glory Girl and I will team up," I say. "We'll take the city."

"Very well," Wind Walker says. "We will search the forest." He steps forward and shakes our hands. "Good hunting my friends."

"Find that cube," Aries says, flashing a grin. "Don't let us find it first."

"You're on," I say.

Then, we watch the heroes run the other away.

Grace 2 reaches out her arms. "May I?"

"You may," I answer, turning around.

Grace 2 puts her arms beneath my armpits, and locks her fingers across my chest. She gathers herself, and then we're off—flying through the harsh climate.

The change in weather is abrupt. One second, we're being battered by fierce winds and driving snow, the next we're being tickled by a warm, gentle mist. I've never seen anything like it. And it's not just the weather.

Over the mountains, just as Grace 2 said there would be, is a sprawling city—five times bigger than Keystone City and at least twice the size of Manhattan. Buildings of all shapes and sizes extend for miles, disappearing at the horizon. At first, it seems like your everyday run-of-the-mill city, but as we pull closer I pick up strange differences in architecture. Like, all the windows are circular instead of square, and the streets are curvy instead of straight.

There must be thousands of buildings, streets, and alleyways down there. And, somewhere, possibly hidden in this vast urban jungle, is a silver cube smaller than a bread box.

Awesome.

We land in the middle of a large intersection when I realize something I failed to notice before—there aren't any cars. Or buses. Or … people.

Where are all the people?

"It's like a ghost town," Grace 2 says.

"Somehow, that's not reassuring," I say. "Now how the heck are we supposed to find the Building Block? We can't look in every single building. There's got to be a better way."

"I've got an idea," Grace 2 says, staring into space.

"Great, lay it on me," I say, relieved at least one of us is thinking clearly on how to start looking for this thing.

"Well," Grace 2 says, "maybe we ought to ask *him*?"

Him? I spin around to see who she's looking at.

In the distance, there's a large, green object hanging off the side of a building. At first, it looks like one of those creepy gargoyle statues, you know, the ones that serve as water spouts or something. And I was pretty good with that explanation … until it unfurls a pair of gigantic bat-like wings.

And then I realize it isn't a statue at all.

We watch as the creature rises to full height, extending several stories taller than first appeared possible. It opens its red eyes, pounds it's chest, and bellows something awful. Then, I realize I've had the misfortune of seeing this creature before.

And this time, I might not be so lucky.

"Run!" I yell, as it leaps from its perch.

Grace 2 takes to the air, while I bolt through the front door of the nearest building I can reach. I cruise through the lobby, leap over a desk, and duck behind it, my heart pounding out of my chest.

That's no gargoyle!

That's a Skelton. And not just any old Skelton. That's a Blood Bringer—the worst kind of Skelton.

Blood Bringers are an elite killing force that can change into any form imaginable. And I'm pretty sure this one knows I'm the guy that blew up an entire squadron of his buddies, along with the Orb of Oblivion.

Or, at least that's what I thought I did. Because, apparently, the Orb isn't so easy to get rid of.

Suddenly, a small insect buzzes over the desk, and lands by my foot.

What tripped me up last time was that the Blood Bringers were armored in Sheelds—those clam-like creatures whose skin is resistant to the Orb's powers.

The bug hops onto my foot and stares at me with its large, green eyes.

Two thoughts come to mind. One, this entire planet is empty, except for us. And two, I've got a long, long history with green-eyed bugs.

I stay as still as a log.

And then I swat down with all my might!

The bug darts safely out of harm's way, and then transforms into the largest Skelton I've ever seen—a seven foot tall specimen of pure ugly. He stares me down with his piercing neon-green eyes and says, "You will have to excuse me, but I find it hard to believe *you* are the one responsible for the death of my brothers."

Here we go again.

"Nevertheless, it is my duty to avenge them. Perhaps I should introduce myself. I am the Destroyer of Worlds, the Harbinger of Death. I am the High Commander of the Blood Bringers. The new High Commander."

Of course he is.

I quickly scan his body up and down, and realize I'm pretty much doomed. Just as I feared, he's covered head-to-toe in leathery brown armor. I'd know that texture anywhere—it's Sheeld—probably standard issue for them now. So even if I wanted to use the Orb of Oblivion—which I don't—I couldn't.

But I still have my powers.

"Sorry to disappoint," I say, "but you won't be avenging anybody today." I concentrate hard, and bathe him with my negation powers.

"Ridiculous child," he says, advancing towards me. "Prepare to—" Then he stops, and realizes something's wrong. He tries and tries, but can't transform his body into anything. "What did you do?" he says.

I cross my arms and smile. "So, tell me, what do you think of me now?"

The High Commander lets out a deafening war cry, and lunges towards me. I dive out of the way as he crashes into the desk behind me, shattering it to pieces.

Even though he's powerless, he's still capable of crushing me. I need to get out of here and find Grace 2! I need her help!

As he rises, I hustle out of the building and back to the main street. Grace 2 spots me from up high, and floats down to meet me.

"Where'd you go?" she says. "I've been looking all over for you!"

"Fly in my soup," I say. "Now let's get out of here!"

Suddenly, the entire façade of the building explodes outwards, blowing Grace 2 and me onto our backsides.

When the dust clears, the High Commander stands before us. "No more games, child," he says. "Now is the time for rev—Ahhhhhhh!"

Suddenly, the High Commander drops to his knees, grabbing his head.

"Get away from them!" comes a female voice.

We turn to find a woman in black standing behind us.

It's Mom!

"I brought them into this world," she says, "and I'll be the one to take them out."

Meta Profile

Name: High Commander
Role: Villain   Status: Active

VITALS:

Race: Skelton
Real Name: Unknown
Height: 7'0"
Weight: 350 lbs
Eye Color: Green
Hair Color: Bald

META POWERS:

Class: Meta-morph
Power Level: ▮▮▮

- Extreme Shape-Shifting—can assume endless forms
- Extreme Flight, Strength, and Speed depending upon form taken

CHARACTERISTICS:

Combat	100	
Durability	100	
Leadership	100	
Strategy	100	
Willpower	100	

THIRTEEN

I SEEM TO BE A GLUTTON FOR PUNISHMENT

It's really great seeing Mom again.

There's just one problem, she's trying to kill me.

Mom 2 has already knocked the High Commander out of commission—and he's on her team! We need to act fast because she's a psychic, and psychics are known for—

"Aaahhh!" Grace 2 screams, dropping to the ground holding her head.

Too late! Mom 2's got her!

But why not me?

"Elliott," she says, "Why are you fighting with those heroes? And what happened to your hair?"

My hair? I'm confused for a second, and then I realize she has no clue about mirror universes. She thinks

I'm Elliott 2—her blond, villainous son from her world!

Maybe I can use it to my advantage?

Grace 2 is squirming, clearly in a world of pain.

"Just a big mix-up, Mom," I say, standing up.

"That's what I thought," she says. "So, do you want to finish her off, or should I?"

Finish her off? That's her own kid!

"I-I h-hate y-you!" Grace 2 sputters out.

"I'll do it," I say quickly, before Mom 2 gets trigger happy. I need to make my move now, before she realizes I'm not who she thinks I am. But how am I going to stop her without risking Grace 2's life? I can't act faster than Mom 2 can think! I mean, it takes me a few seconds to get my own powers going! By then, she may turn Grace 2 into a vegetable!

"Now's our chance," comes a voice in my head.

What? Oh no.

"It's our only chance to save her life," it says.

"What are you waiting for?" Mom 2 asks. "Do it!"

Grace 2 is writhing on the ground. She screams out again. Mom 2 must really be turning the screws.

"Don't ruin this for me, Elliott," Mom 2 says. "You're already the ruler of Earth. When we win, I get my own planet to rule."

Grace 2 stares at me, her eyes pleading.

I have no other choice.

"Use me," the Orb says.

"Who's that?" Mom 2 says, snapping her head my

way. "Wait ... you're not my son!"

"*Orb,*" I command. "*Knock her out. Now!*"

Suddenly, Mom 2 screams, and then falls to the ground like a limp noodle.

"No, Mom," I say. "I'm not."

"W-what happened?" Grace 2 says groggily. "Did you do that?"

I slump to the ground, exhausted.

"*And now we're one,*" the Orb says. "*Now we're fully one.*"

Which is exactly what I was afraid of.

"Elliott, are you okay?" Grace 2 asks, sliding over, and putting her hand on my shoulder.

"I'm not sure," I say. The last time the Orb and I were connected, I was able to use my willpower to completely master it. But this time, it feels different—like we're sharing space in my brain—like I'm not alone. "I just need a minute."

"I think she was really going to kill me this time," she says. "You saved my life."

"No problem," I say. "I didn't realize your mom was so evil. It was ... shocking."

"Tell me about it," she says. "I've been dealing with it since I was little. Dad tried to protect me from her, but I guess you can't always shield the ones you love. But even I didn't realize how deep her madness ran. I guess I do now."

"I'm so sorry," I say.

"It's not your fault," Grace 2 says. "At least there's

some comfort knowing she's a good person on your world."

"The best," I say. Suddenly, I feel an overwhelming wave of emotion. Images of my family flash through my mind. I don't think I've ever missed them more than I do right now.

"Hey," Grace 2 says, putting her arms around me. "We'll get through this. Together."

I smile, and wipe my eyes. Even though I don't have my family here, Grace 2 is the next best thing. "C'mon," I say. "Let's find that stupid cube. We've got a planet to save."

We lock hands, and pull each other up. Mom 2 and the High Commander are still out, and I don't want to be hanging around when they wake up. We've got to find the Building Block, and even though I don't like it, I know what I need to do.

"Orb," I think. *"Can you locate the Building Block?"*

"The cube is a cosmic entity," it replies. *"I can sense it's energy, but can't pinpoint it's exact location. We need to travel further north."*

Well, that's better than nothing, so I tell Grace 2 I've got a hunch. She wraps her arms around me, and we take off again.

I feel guilty not telling her about the Orb, but I don't want to freak her out either. After all, I think it's the Orb that corrupted her brother. So, telling her may cloud her trust in me. Especially with the war being waged inside my head right now.

"Why don't we end this silly game," the Orb says.

"Shut up," I reply.

"We can do that," it says, *"we don't need Order or Chaos. We can make our own destiny. Together."*

"Stay focused," I command. *"And please, stop talking."*

"You don't want to know where the cube is?" it asks.

"Of course I want to know where the stupid cube is," I say.

"Then I guess I'll keep talking."

And it's like this the rest of the way—the Orb yammers on and on about "destiny" and "ruling the universe." I try to ignore it, to treat it like background noise, but it's not easy when you can't turn it off.

We're in the air for a long time, and Grace 2 is noticeably tired from lugging me such a long way. We pass through several more changes in scenery—islands, grasslands, swamp—and every time it's like crossing some abrupt, imaginary divide.

And then we enter a desert.

"The Building Block is hidden here," the Orb says.

White sands spread out beneath us for miles. It's hot—oppressively hot—with not even the hint of a breeze. Beads of sweat form on my forehead and trickle down the back of my neck. Strangely, the landscape is almost beautiful here, if you weren't fighting for survival.

Grace 2's loft lowers noticeably, the harsh climate sapping her strength. We'd better be close, because I'm not sure she's going to make it much farther.

And then, up ahead, I see it, rising above the sea of whiteness into the burning sky—a giant pyramid. At first, it seems like a mirage—an optical illusion conjured up by my tired brain. But, as we get closer I know it's real. I studied ancient Egypt and its pyramid's in school, but I've never seen a real one before. It's truly an engineering marvel—triangular in shape, and faced on all sides with polished, green limestone.

"The artifact is inside the pyramid," the Orb says.

"We've found it!" I yell to Grace 2. "It's in there!"

She whoops with delight.

But our celebration is short-lived, because there are three small dots at the base of the pyramid—only one of which is moving. Someone is waiting for us—next to a pair of bodies lying in the sand.

It's Siphon! And the bodies are Aries and Wind Walker!

And then I remember Siphon's powers.

"Pull up!" I shout. "Pull up!"

But, it's too late. Just as Grace 2 changes course, a black void opens in front of us, swallowing us whole!

Suddenly, we're flying through a pitch black tunnel. The space around us is narrowing, closing in quickly. There's a powerful headwind pushing against us, like we're going the wrong way through a vacuum cleaner hose! And then, with a loud POP, we tumble headfirst out the other side.

My mouth fills with sand. I try scrambling to my feet,

but lose my footing, landing on top of something hard. Lifting my head, I'm face-to-face with an unconscious Wind Walker! Thankfully, he's breathing. Then it dawns on me what happened. Siphon must have used Wind Walker's powers to yank us clear out of the sky! Aries is lying beside us, knocked out, but clearly breathing, too.

I check on Grace 2, who's bent over by the base of the pyramid, tossing her cookies.

I'm the only one in fighting shape.

Fan-freaking-tastic.

I move to stand up, when the area around me darkens in a large shadow.

"Sorry about your friends," Siphon says. "They took out Overlord, so they didn't do too badly. But, unfortunately for them, I'm on a completely different level."

I don't think truer words have been spoken. The last time we met, my negation powers didn't work at all on him. But this time, I'm not alone. I've got the Orb of Oblivion.

I look into Siphon's eyes, but surprisingly, his expression isn't threatening. Something tells me to hold back.

"The Building Block is inside the pyramid," Siphon says matter-of-factly. "There's a secret door on the outside, leading to a maze of passages. Once you reach the main chamber, the Building Block's inside the pharaoh's sarcophagus. Seems kind of fitting, doesn't it?"

I stare at him, baffled. "If you know all this, why didn't you grab it? You'd win the contest. You'd have your own planet to rule?"

"Oh, believe me," he says, "I considered it. But when I learned you were one of my opponents, I couldn't believe my luck. From that moment, game or no game, destroying you became my number one priority. I decided that even if I found the Building Block before finding you, I'd wait to win the game. That way, I wouldn't miss my chance for revenge before we were transported off this crazy world."

Seriously? This guy is nuts! "I told you," I say, rising cautiously. "I didn't kill your father. It was the Skelton."

"Yeah, you did say that," Siphon says. "But the High Commander tells a different story."

The High Commander? I forgot! Siphon and the High Commander have been partners on Chaos' team for days! I need to think fast.

"And you believed him?" I ask, making it to my feet, shocked he let me stand at all without taking my head off.

And then I realize something.

If he wanted to kill me so badly, why hasn't he done it by now? My Mom's words echo in my brain: *Never judge a book by its cover.* Just because he looks like Meta-Taker, doesn't mean he acts like Meta-Taker. Then, I get an idea.

"You know, villains like the High Commander are notorious for lying. And so was your father."

"What?" Siphon says angrily.

Okay, tread carefully. Think this through.

"When we first met, you said your father isolated you," I continue. "Which got me thinking—was he really protecting you from others, like he told you? Or was he keeping you from finding out the truth about who he really was?"

"What are you talking about?" Siphon says.

"Did you know your father wasn't just a villain, but he was the worst kind of villain—a cold-blooded murderer?"

"Liar!" Siphon yells. "My father did what needed to be done! To make a life for both of us! If someone needed to be destroyed, there was a reason for it!"

"No, Siphon," I say. "He murdered innocents—and he murdered often. In fact, you might not know this, but he murdered five members of the original Freedom Force—good people—heroes. You may be his son, but I don't think you're like him. In fact, I don't think you're like him at all. If you were, wouldn't you have killed me by now?"

Siphon is frozen. I can see the wheels spinning in his brain. It's working!

"Use me!" the Orb says inside my mind. *"Use me now!"*

"Shut up!" I command. *"Not now!"*

Suddenly, Siphon's eyes ignite with swirling, red energy. "What's this?" he says, astonished. "What's all of this power I feel coming off of you. You're trying to trick me. You're setting me up!"

"Go dark!" I yell to the Orb in my mind. *"Now!"*

"My father was right," Siphon says, "I can't trust anybody!"

"No," I say. "That's not true."

Siphon's red energy kicks into overdrive. Suddenly, I feel drained. Like all of my energy is leaving me.

Siphon's body starts to swell, growing larger and larger as he draws more and more power away from me ... and into him!

"Orb?" I call into my mind.

But there's no answer.

"Are you there, Orb? Talk to me?"

Nothing.

I look back at Siphon whose ballooned in size. He's like a cartoon of himself, bloated and deformed. "The power," he mutters. "Such unbelievable power ... "

I need to get away from Siphon—to draw the Orb's power away of him! But then—

"BOOM!" comes a deafening sound from above.

I look up to find a silver, sleek-looking ship with a long, cylindrical body hovering in the sky.

The Ghost Ship! But how?

"KABOOM!" comes an even more thunderous noise overhead, knocking me to my knees, and sending my ears ringing.

Looking up, I find the Ghost Ship surrounded by a fleet of ships. Skelton warships.

The Emperor has found me.

Meta Profile

Name: Ms. Understood (2)
Role: Villain   Status: Active

VITALS:

Race: Human
Real Name: Kate Harkness
Height: 5'6"
Weight: 130 lbs
Eye Color: Brown
Hair Color: Blond

META POWERS:

Class: Psychic
Power Level: ▮▮▮

- Extreme Telepathy
- Extreme Telekinesis
- Group Mind-Linking
- Long-Range Capability

CHARACTERISTICS:

Combat	80	
Durability	42	
Leadership	88	
Strategy	85	
Willpower	95	

FOURTEEN

I LEARN WHY OPPOSITES ATTRACT

It's just another day at the office for your friendly neighborhood super-zero.

I'm fighting for my life in the middle of a desert, Grace 2 is still recovering from our psychedelic roller-coaster ride, Aries and Wind Walker are comatose, Siphon seems to have sucked the Orb of Oblivion's power into his body, and the Zodiac are being chased by an armada of Skelton warships.

Oh, and I almost forgot to mention the Building Block—the whole reason we're stuck on this crazy planet in the first place—which is sitting inside the tomb of an ancient pharaoh, just waiting for someone to grab it.

I seriously should consider a different line of work. One where my life isn't at stake every second—like dentistry.

But that'll have to wait, because right now I've got to get my act together.

At the moment, Siphon is distracted by the aerial fireworks happening overhead. I could make a run for the Building Block, but there's no way I'd get two feet before he creamed me. I need a game plan, but at this point I'm flat out of ideas.

Just then, the Ghost Ship slams to the ground, skidding hundreds of feet in the sand before coming to a stop. The hatch pops open, and out jump a host of friendly faces. Gemini, Taurus, Pisces, Scorpio, and Sagittarius! And, of course, my old pal, Leo.

They see me, and start running towards us!

"Stop!" I yell. "Stay back!"

The Zodiac freeze in their tracks. Thank goodness! I couldn't imagine adding even more powers to Siphon's growing arsenal.

Suddenly, dozens of Skelton warships touch down around us. But before we can organize, ramps deploy and hundreds of Blood Bringers swarm out. Within seconds, we're surrounded!

The Blood Bringers are as big as I remember— sumo-sized warriors clad in armor and carrying deadly spear-like weapons. Just then, a group parts in the center, creating a pathway for a Skelton wearing a gold cape and crown.

The Emperor!

He looks down at me with his neon-green eyes,

grinning from pointy ear to pointy ear. "So, Orb Master, we meet again. You seem to have forgotten you are my prisoner."

I have to admit, he's even more intimidating in person. He's tall, broad shouldered, and has a sinister quality to his face that makes you think someone's about to stick a dagger in your back. Which probably isn't too far from the truth.

"Sorry about that," I say. "Something came up."

I realize that standing before me is the most feared man in the universe, responsible for orchestrating countless acts of death and destruction. He ordered the murders of K'ami and her father. He endorsed what happened to all the villains who lost their lives at Lockdown—including Siphon's father.

I turn to catch Siphon's eye, but he's gone!

Where'd he go?

Instinctively, I look towards the pyramid, only to find Siphon stepping out of one of Wind Walker's rifts! He feels delicately along the pyramid's stone exterior, and then pushes through a secret door. He's going for the Building Block!

I've got to stop him. But first I need to solve my present conundrum.

The Emperor looks me squarely in the eyes. "Grab the boy," he orders to his minions. "Dispose of the rest."

The Skelton charge forward!

Suddenly, they're on me, pulling my arms behind my

back, and lifting me off the ground! The next thing I know, I'm dropped in front of the Emperor!

"No more games, Orb Master," the Emperor says. "Now you will pay for running away by watching your friends die."

The Zodiac spring into action, but the Blood Bringers use their shape-shifting powers to transform into a horde of horrific creatures. Scorpio and Sagittarius fend off multi-headed beasts and tentacled monsters. Gemini and Taurus scatter an army of scampering scorpion creatures. Pisces is being chased by a flock of winged, frog-like things. And I have no clue where Leo is. It's only a matter of time before they're overrun.

But I need to catch Siphon!

Scorpio disappears under a pile of muscled rodents.

I need to act now, before it's too late! I may not have the Orb's power, but I still have mine. I think all the way back to my mission with the Destruction Crew—the one that got me kicked off the Freedom Force.

If I can use my powers to stop the Blood Bringers, it should be easy for the Zodiac to do the rest. But, what if I mistakenly wipe out everyone's powers again? They'd be doomed! But, if I don't try, they're doomed anyway!

For some reason, I hear Grace 2's words in my head: *you can't always shield the ones you love.*

Maybe, just maybe …

I close my eyes, and focus harder than I've ever focused before. I push my negation powers as far and as wide as I can. But this time, I picture all of the heroes in my mind: Scorpio, Sagittarius, Gemini, Pisces, Taurus, Grace 2, Wind Walker, Aries—even Leo—and I wrap them in a mental shield—protecting them from the effects of my powers. And then I pray. Please work, please work, please—

"What is happening?" cries the Emperor.

I open my eyes, and do a double take! All of the terrifying creatures are gone! And, in their places stand hundreds of confused Blood Bringers.

I … did it?

"Zodiac!" Scorpio yells. "Attack!"

And then Scorpio's tail turns bright orange, and he fires a laser blast straight through the heart of the Blood Bringer army!

Yes! The Zodiac still have their powers! I did it!

The Emperor turns to me, fuming with anger, "Take him to the ship!"

But before they can move, I feel two hands grab me beneath my armpits, and lift me high into the air.

"Grace!" I yell.

"I figure I owed you one," she says, winking.

"Quick," I say, "drop me by the near side of the pyramid. Siphon's inside. I've got to stop him."

"Signed, sealed, and delivered," she says, picking up speed, and depositing me at the exact spot. "Go get him!"

But I don't have time to respond. I've got to get to the Building Block! I start pushing the area of the wall I saw Siphon touching. There's a secret door around here somewhere. Finally, I hear a CLICK, and a door swings inwards. I jump inside.

It's dark. So dark, that when my eyes adjust I can only see a few feet in front of my face. I don't have the luxury to go back out and see if I can borrow a flashlight. So, I take off, spreading my arms and using the sides of the walls to guide me as I move forward. I'm running blind, but that's the best I can do.

The passageway ends abruptly, and I smack into a stone wall. Decision time. I can either go left or right. I follow my instincts, and turn right. This happens over and over again. Hit a dead end, pick a side, and just keep going.

This whole process is taking too long. I feel like a rat in a maze, with no clue how to find the cheese—which, in this case, is the pharaoh's tomb. Siphon told me he already found his way to the main chamber once, so I've got to assume he's reached the Building Block by now.

So why hasn't the game ended already?

I smash face-first into yet another wall, and then turn left. I hustle ten feet or so when, suddenly, everything opens up. Smooth, granite walls meet symmetrically overhead. Light streams through a small hole in the middle of the ceiling. Within the center of the chamber lies an open, granite sarcophagus.

I've found it! But where's—

"I couldn't do it," comes a voice to my left.

I spin to find Siphon sitting in the corner of the room. He looks sad.

"A voice in my head kept telling me to grab it," he says. "Just grab the Building Block, and then I'd be the ruler of my own world. But then I thought about what you said, and you were right. Deep down I knew exactly who my father was. And I'm not like him. I'm not a murderer. I could never kill billions of innocent people just to get what I want."

I can't believe my ears. He actually listened to me!

"I'm sorry," I say. "Look, I know that was hard, but I'm glad you made the decision you did. You did the right thing. You know, that kind of makes you a hero now."

Siphon looks at me strangely and laughs. "Me? A hero? Who would've thought? Anyway, the Building Block's in there. You take it. Let's go home already."

I smile, and head over to the sarcophagus. I look inside, expecting to find a decrepit mummy, but instead there's just a silver cube—the Building Block!

Finally, this is all going to end.

"I wouldn't touch that if I were you," comes a high-pitched voice.

I turn to see a tall man with purple skin floating down from above. His hair is white and wild, like a raging inferno. He's wearing a black, leather jacket, and faded blue jeans, riddled with holes. He lowers his sunglasses, looking at me with contempt. There's no need for introductions. I know him immediately—it's Chaos!

"Your side cheated," he says. "So, I win." Then he reaches inside and takes the Building Block.

"Hey," I exclaim. "You can't do that!"

Cheated? What's he talking about. What's going on?

Suddenly, Order appears on the other side of the sarcophagus. "You lost fair and square, brother, and, as usual, you are having a difficult time accepting the fact."

"Enough of your drama," Chaos says. "It exhausts me. You violated the rules by bringing participants into the contest who were not selected—which is also known as cheating."

Watching them argue is like watching two gods bicker over a game of chess. Except we're the pawns!

"I did no such thing," Order continues. "These so-called 'participants' you are referring to happened upon Arena World by chance. I had nothing to do with it."

"Blah, blah, blah," Chaos says, rolling his eyes. "You never have anything to do with it, do you? You have forfeited the match. The world is now rightfully mine to destroy. And destroy it I shall!"

"Enough, Chaos!" Order thunders. "The only thing that will be destroyed is you!" Order points at his brother, and suddenly, the Building Block in Chaos' hands starts glowing!

"What are you doing?" Chaos exclaims.

"You are so predictable, brother," Order says. "By grabbing the Building Block, you are now locked to this place. Or have you forgotten?"

Chaos' expression changes to one of surprise. He looks down at the Building Block. "Release me at once!"

"No, brother," Order says. "You and I are the highest of all cosmic beings. And, as it is written in the stars, we are unable to do harm upon one another. But that does not mean we cannot be harmed."

"Are you mad, brother!" Chaos says.

"Perhaps," Order says. "But if I am, it is you who made me so. Just like the Orb of Oblivion, the Building Block is a cosmic entity—a parasite—that feeds off the desires of its host. But while the Orb of Oblivion brings out the darkness, the Building Block brings out the light. And, resting in your vile hands, it is reversing your powers, even as we speak. So, tell me brother. Do you feel your power slipping away? Do you feel yourself growing weaker and weaker by the second?"

Wait? Order said the Building Block was a living entity, but he never said it was the opposite of the Orb— that it's a cosmic force for good!

Suddenly, Chaos starts shrinking! "S-stop ... p-please!"

"Like you and I," Order continues, "the Building Block and Orb of Oblivion are opposite sides of the same coin. But while our purpose is to provide harmony, their purpose is to provide dissonance. And when they connect, the results can be rather ... explosive."

O! M! G! This is what he meant when he said: *When the appropriate moment arises, you will act.* He's going to use the Orb to blow Chaos sky high!

"Now that you are sufficiently weakened, brother" Order says, "it is time to rid ourselves of the burden of Chaos! Come forth, Orb Master!" Order says looking at me, an evil grin spreading across his face. "Come forth and claim your prize!"

Order snaps. But instead of me, it's Siphon who lifts off the ground!

"Hey!" Siphon exclaims.

"What is this?" Order exclaims.

What's going on?

Then it hits me! When Siphon absorbed my powers, he just didn't take the Orb's powers from me—he took the entire Orb of Oblivion! No wonder it wasn't talking to me!

Siphon flies towards Chaos, but Chaos uses whatever power he has left to push Siphon back, keeping him away.

Siphon is now hovering between the cosmic brothers.

"Epic Zero, run!" Siphon yells.

"No!" I yell. "I'll help you!"

"Remember what you said," Siphon says. "Remember me as a hero."

"Do not do this, fool," Chaos says. "You need me!"

"Do I?" Order chuckles. "I am Order, and Order needs no one!"

"Want to know what I think?" Siphon interjects. "I think you guys deserve each other!"

Suddenly, Siphon reaches out and grabs Order's arm.

"What are you doing?" Order yells.

They both start glowing.

"Since I've got this Orb thing," Siphon says. "I guess now you're frozen, too!"

"Unhand me, fool!" Order yells.

I watch Siphon then reach out for Chaos' arm.

Order's eyes grow wide. "Stop! What are you—"

"NO!" Chaos yells.

But before he clutches Chaos' wrist, Siphon looks at me, and raises his eyebrows.

And I'm swallowed up in a black rift.

***

I fall out the other side into the desert sand.

The explosion is other-worldly.

A wave of pure white energy eclipses the sky.

And then everything goes dark.

When my eyes readjust, there's no trace of the pyramid. Order, Chaos, and Siphon are gone—all in the blink of an eye.

Siphon ported me out of there with one of Wind Walker's rifts. Siphon sacrificed himself to save … me?

Suddenly, the ground starts shaking violently.

Then, it CRACKS open, sending a plume of hot lava shooting into the air.

Arena World is falling apart!

I lock eyes with the Emperor, who's being helped to his feet by his henchmen. He stares at me, and then shouts, "Retreat!"

I nod my thanks, and watch as he leads his men back to their ships.

"To the Ghost Ship!" Gemini yells. "Hurry!"

Taurus heaves Aries over her shoulder, while Scorpio lifts Wind Walker onto Sagittarius' backside. Grace 2 swoops down and grabs me, right as another crack opens beneath my feet.

"Thanks," I say.

"No problem" she says. "It's what heroes do."

We all tumble into the Ghost Ship, taking off just before the ground disintegrates beneath it. I know we need to get as far away from here as possible, but there's one thing we need to take care of first.

I push my way to the cockpit, and find Scorpio. "We need to make a stop," I say.

Within seconds we're there.

The ground is shaking like mad, and buildings are collapsing around us, but we need to do this.

The hatch lowers and Grace 2 flies out. Seconds later, she returns with her unconscious mom in her arms.

Then, we blast off into outer space as Arena World bursts into a ball of fire and rubble.

Meta Profile

Name: The Emperor
Role: Villain   Status: Active

VITALS:

Race: Skelton
Real Name: Unknown
Height: 6'6"
Weight: 275 lbs
Eye Color: Green
Hair Color: Bald

META POWERS:

Class: Meta-morph
Power Level: ▊▊▊▊

- Assumed Extreme Shape-Shifting—can morph into endless forms
- Assumed Extreme Flight, Strength, and Speed depending upon form taken

CHARACTERISTICS:

Combat	100	▊▊▊▊
Durability	100	▊▊▊▊
Leadership	100	▊▊▊▊
Strategy	100	▊▊▊▊
Willpower	100	▊▊▊▊

FIFTEEN

I PUT MY TRUST IN A MONKEY

We're all in our heads.

Other than Pisces and Scorpio, who are navigating the Ghost Ship, no one's talking. I know I'm still trying to process everything that happened, and I've got more questions than answers.

Like, why did Siphon sacrifice himself for me? Believe me, I'm grateful, but I can't help feeling partly responsible. I mean, I told him the truth about his father, but I suspect deep down he already knew. He had no family—no one to go back home to. I think he wanted to make up for his father's mistakes, and this was his chance to rewrite his family's legacy. So, he made the ultimate sacrifice, and for that, he'll always be a hero in my book.

And then, there's the question of what happens now without Order and Chaos? When I met Order he told me that he and his brother were the fabric of the universe. So, what happens when that fabric is shredded to pieces? If Order managed structure, and Chaos managed randomness, what's going to happen to the universe now that they're gone—all of the universes?

And then I get a more horrifying thought.

Who's going to control Ravager?

Without Order and Chaos, there's no longer a contest. And without a contest, there aren't any restrictions as to what that planet-eating pest can do. So, does that mean the Earth we nearly died saving may be at risk again tomorrow?

Suddenly, I feel nauseous.

And then, of course, there's the Orb of Oblivion. I keep trying to reach out to it, but there's just no response. Did it truly die with Siphon? Or, is it somehow still inside of me, gathering it's strength? Even though I can't sense it's presence, can I ever be entirely sure it's gone?

I rest my throbbing head against the hull of the ship.

Grace 2 enters from the medi-wing. "Thanks again, Elliott. Saving my mom's life was a really honorable thing to do."

"No problem," I say. "You would have done the same for me. How's she doing?"

"She's still unconscious," Grace 2 says. "But Leo says she's stable. He thinks she's going to make a full recovery. Wind Walker and Aries are back on their feet."

"Yeah, I heard the cheers when Aries realized he was

back on the Ghost Ship. Do you think you're gonna be okay? You know, with your mom? I imagine that's gonna be a tough thing to get over."

She looks at her feet. "I don't know. She's still my mom, you know? I hope she realizes how far gone she is, and can make her way back. I know I won't ever forget, but maybe, one day, I'll be able to forgive. How about you?"

"I don't know how I feel," I say. "Everything that happened back there was so crazy. I just really want to get home, you know?"

She reaches out and rubs my shoulder, a sharp pain shoots down my left arm. "Ow!" I cry.

"You're hurt," she says. "Sorry, I didn't know."

"Honestly, neither did I," I say, my arm still smarting. "It must have happened when everything blew up. I was running on so much adrenaline I didn't even notice."

"Leo's still in the medi-wing," Grace 2 says. "Maybe he should look at it."

"Yeah, that's probably a good idea," I say, pulling myself up. My arm is really sore, I hope nothing's broken.

When I enter the medi-wing, Mom 2 is lying on a table hooked up to a bunch of machines monitoring her vital signs. My favorite monkey is scrolling through a computer screen, a clipboard tucked under his hairy arm.

"Hey, Leo," I say. "Can you take a look at me? It's my left arm."

The chimp turns, and hesitates for a moment, like he's surprised to see me. Then he grins and pats the empty examination table. "Sure, I'd be happy to."

I hop up, careful not to bump my left arm on anything. Leo's behind me, making a racket as he collects some equipment. Then I realize there's something I've been meaning to ask him.

"Hey, I know we didn't get off on the right foot, but there's something bothering me that I haven't been able to piece together."

"Sure, what is it" he says, clanging behind me.

"Scorpio told me the Zodiac only found me because of you. But, I have no idea how you did it. I mean, how did you even know about the Orb?"

"Ah," Leo says. "I see. Perhaps an explanation is in order. But first, I need to do this."

THWIP!

Ouch! There's a sharp pain in my left shoulder! I turn to find Leo standing beside me, holding a small gun.

What the—? He tranquilized me!

"You'll soon be quite groggy," Leo says, swinging around the table to the door. "But I'm sure you're familiar with the feeling." He turns the latch, locking it shut!

What's going on? Everything starts getting blurry. I'm trapped inside with a psychotic primate whose trying to kill me!

Suddenly, he's standing in front of me. "Perhaps this

will help to explain things." And then, before my eyes, he transforms from a chimpanzee into a boy—an alien boy with pale-yellow skin, and large, pointy ears. And then he reaches up and pinches his pupils, removing brown contact lenses to reveal a pair of neon-green eyes.

He's ... he's ...

"I can tell from your astonished expression that you realize I am a Skelton. My name is K'van Sollarr, younger brother of K'ami Sollarr. I think you knew her well before leading her to her death."

What? K'ami has a brother? She never mentioned a brother. By now, I'm struggling to stay conscious. I want to call for help, but I'm having trouble even holding myself upright. He must have drugged me twice as heavily as before.

"Perhaps she never told you about me, but I am not surprised. We never did get along. You see, I am the last of the Sollarr line, and the only one loyal to our Lord Emperor. As for how I found you ... "

Now he's loading a syringe with some kind of serum.

"You may be aware that Skelton of the same blood lines share a psychic bond—a mind-link if you will. Once my sister touched the Orb of Oblivion, I was, by association, directly connected with you. As soon as I realized this wonderful development, I informed the Emperor. You can probably imagine that after the treasonous acts of my father and sister, it took quite a bit of convincing for the Emperor to believe me. But after I held true through all of his torture sessions, he was finally convinced."

Suddenly, my left arm is on fire! He's rubbing something on it!

"He sent me alone to Earth to track you down. Given how you destroyed an entire Blood Bringer squadron, he was reluctant to risk more resources until you were found. I admit it took me longer than I expected. Your satellite was not obvious, and I spent weeks fruitlessly searching your planet's surface."

Leo grabs my left arm! The pain!

"Unfortunately, my ship was out of fuel, and I needed a way back into space to reach you. Fortunately, Canada had a secret space launch planned. They were sending a chimpanzee into orbit. The night before the launch, I infiltrated their building, and took the place of their astronaut. After liftoff, I charted my own course, but your rockets are so primitive I quickly ran out of fuel. Fortunately, the Zodiac heeded my distress call. They are a ragtag band of misfits, so it was child's play to convince them the Orb was the answer to their prayers to defeat the mighty Ravager, and avenge their worlds. Once aboard, I used the Ghost Ship's capabilities to track you down and land undetected on your satellite. The rest, they say, is history."

Then everything clicks. That's why he didn't want to turn me over to the Overlord!

"You ... called the Skelton Emperor ... on Watcher

World," I mutter.

"Yes, I did," he says. "And I thought that would be the end of it. I'd deliver you into the hands of the Emperor, clear my family's name, and my people would rule the universe—with me, of course, in a dangerously close position to the Emperor. But now the Orb is gone, so I need a new plan. And, at this point, there is really no need for you to blow my cover. I do enjoy manipulating these kids, and I have a few more tricks up my sleeve. So, I guess you just came down with a serious case of heart attack."

I feel a sharp pinch on my arm. He's putting the syringe in! He's going to kill me!

"Drop the needle!" comes a familiar voice.

I manage to open my eyes to find a woman's dark, gloved hand wrapped around Leo's wrist. And then, I watch—Mom?—sock the villain square across the jaw!

And then I'm out.

***

"Elliott?"

When I come to, I'm surrounded by concerned faces. The Zodiac are there, as are Grace 2, and Wind Walker. Gemini is squeezing my hand tightly.

"He's okay," she says. "Thank the stars."

I'm still groggy. I try to sit up, but there's something in the way. My left arm is in a cast!

"Leo!" I say, "Leo's—"

"No longer a problem," Grace 2 says. "Thanks to my mom."

Then I remember everything. At first, I thought just Leo and I were in the medi-wing. But Mom 2 was also there! She was on that table. She saved my life.

Grace 2 steps aside, and her Mom is standing there, smiling. "I'm glad you're okay, Elliott," she says. "Despite everything I've done, you came back—you all came back—to rescue me. You reminded me of what it means to be a hero. And for that, I'll never be able to thank you enough." I watch as she reaches out for Grace 2's hand.

Grace 2 hesitates, and then takes it.

"What about Leo?" I ask.

"We tranquilized him, and locked him in the storage closet," Scorpio says. "We're going to swing by Alcan IV, the prison planet, and drop him off there. We had no idea he wasn't who he said he was. I'm so sorry."

"It's not your fault," I say, "I guess it's been an adventure filled with surprises."

"Indeed," Gemini says. And then she plants a kiss on my cheek.

I turn beet red.

"And they just keep on coming," Grace 2 says.

And we all laugh.

Meta Profile

Name: Chaos
Role: Cosmic Entity   Status: Deceased?

VITALS:

Race: Inapplicable
Real Name: Chaos
Height: appears 7'0"
Weight: Unknown
Eye Color: Inapplicable
Hair Color: White

META POWERS:

Class: Inapplicable
Power Level: Incalculable

- Balances his brother, Order, to cause stress, disorder, and randomness throughout the universe

- Cannot harm other Cosmic Entities

CHARACTERISTICS:

Combat	Inapplicable
Durability	Inapplicable
Leadership	Inapplicable
Strategy	Inapplicable
Willpower	Inapplicable

EPILOGUE

THE END OF THE ROAD ...

Going home is bittersweet.

For days it was all I could think about, but now that it's finally here it's hard to say goodbye.

Grace 2 and Mom 2 leave first. Grace 2 and I hug for a long time, both of us with tears in our eyes. Even though we started off on the wrong foot, it's amazing to think of how far we've come. I'm really going to miss her.

Then, her Mom gives me a big hug. I thank her for saving my life, and she thanks me for saving hers—twice. I sure hope she lives up to her promises and becomes a hero again. She has lots of damage to undo on her world—especially with her daughter.

I wave goodbye as they each take Wind Walker's hand, and then disappear into his mystical vortex.

Meeting these mirror versions made me realize how

lucky I am to have parents who love me. As for my own Grace, I guess she's not so bad. We love each other, even if we have a funny way of showing it.

When Wind Walker returns, I know I'm next. The Zodiac surround me to say their goodbyes.

"Epic Zero," Scorpio says. "We couldn't have done it without you. And we couldn't imagine moving forward without making you an official member of our team."

"What?" I say. "Really?"

"From this day forward, within our circle, you will be known as Serpentarius—the thirteenth sign of the Zodiac—unifier and healer of worlds."

And then Pisces steps forward and hands me something. It's a badge—a symbol of a serpent!

"That's an official Zodiac communications link," she says, hugging me. "If you ever need us, just push the button and we'll be there."

I turn to the rest of the Zodiac. Taurus wraps me in a giant bear hug, and Sagittarius high-hoofs me. Then, Aries shakes my hand.

"You know," he says, "I really didn't think you'd find the Building Block before me. But you sure proved me wrong."

"What can I say?" I answer. "Good things come in small packages."

He pats me on the shoulder and grins.

And then I meet eyes with Gemini.

She looks really sad. I don't know what it is, but

every time I'm around her I get a funny feeling in my stomach. "I'd love for you to visit my world sometime," I say. "I know it's not your home, but you might like it."

"I'd like that," she says. "But first, I need to finish what I've started. But I'll keep in touch. I promise" Then she gives me a peck on the cheek, and whispers, "See you soon, Elliott."

I feel my cheeks go flush as I join Wind Walker. He takes my hand, and summons one of his mystical voids. I scan the sad faces of the Zodiac one last time, and say, "Goodbye ... team."

And then, they're gone.

Wind Walker leads me through his crazy, dark tunnel, and seconds later, we pop out the other side.

We're in my bedroom—on the Waystation!

Wind Walker puts his hands on my shoulders, and says, "I am glad we are friends, and not foes. Be well, Epic Zero. If you ever need me, you only need to call." And then he conjures up another void, steps inside, and is gone.

I'm finally home. And it feels really weird. The last time I was here, Leo shot me, and that started this whole crazy adventure. I wonder if anyone's around?

I enter the hallway, and everything seems back to normal—there aren't any alarms blaring or barricades in the way. As I make my way up the stairway my mind wanders to everything I've been through. There's no more Orb. No more Order and Chaos. Who knows what the future holds?

I enter the Galley where I find Mom, Grace, and Dog-Gone. Dog-Gone sees me first and charges me at full speed, bowling me over. I wrap my one good arm around his fuzzy neck and pull him close.

"Elliott?" Mom says, running over. "Where have you been? We've been worried sick."

But I can't answer under the barrage of face-licking.

"The entire team is out looking for you," Mom continues. "And what's wrong with your arm? You're in a cast." Mom grabs me and pulls me close. It feels so good to hug her again.

No sooner does she release me, than I'm wrapped up again—this time by Grace, who has a tear in her eye. "I'm glad you're back, squirt," she says. "Just don't crease the cape."

"Elliott, what happened to you?" Mom asks.

But all I can do is stare at them with tears streaming down my face. Normally, I'd be embarrassed, but right now I just don't care. That's my Mom with her brown hair, and my sister with her blond hair.

I'm home.

Grace hands me the end of her cape. "Fine," she sighs, "wipe away."

I dab my eyes. "Boy, do I have a story for you guys. You're never going to believe what happened."

"Can't wait," Grace says. "But do us a favor."

"What's that?" I ask.

"This time, try not to leave out any of the critically important details," she says with a wink.

Mom calls the rest of the Freedom Force back to the Waystation, and it's amazing to see them all again—especially Dad, who hugged me and wouldn't let go.

And then, over jelly doughnuts, I tell them everything.

Well, everything except for Gemini, of course.

I mean, I have to keep some things to myself.

GET MORE EPIC FREE!

Don't miss any of the action! Get a FREE copy of Epic Zero 1.5: Tales of a Serious Superhero Screw Up.

Get your FREE book exclusively from the author's website: rlullman.com.

META POWERS GLOSSARY

FROM THE META MONITOR:
There are nine known Meta power classifications. These classifications have been established to simplify Meta identification and provide a quick framework to understand a Meta's potential powers and capabilities. **Note:** Metas can possess powers in more than one classification. In addition, Metas can evolve over time in both the powers they express, as well as the effectiveness of their powers.

Due to the wide range of Meta abilities, superpowers have been further segmented into power levels. Power levels differ across Meta power classifications. In general, the following power levels have been established:

- Meta 0: Displays no Meta power.
- Meta 1: Displays limited Meta power.
- Meta 2: Displays considerable Meta power.
- Meta 3: Displays extreme Meta power.

The following is a brief overview of the nine Meta power classifications.

ENERGY MANIPULATION:
Energy Manipulation is the ability to generate, shape or act as a conduit, for various forms of energy. Energy Manipulators are able to control energy by focusing or redirecting energy towards a specific target or shaping/reshaping energy for a specific task. Energy Manipulators are often impervious to the forms of energy they are able to manipulate.

Examples of the types of energies utilized by Energy
Manipulators include, but are not limited to:

- Atomic
- Chemical
- Cosmic
- Electricity
- Gravity
- Heat
- Light
- Magnetic
- Sound
- Space
- Time

Note: the fundamental difference between an Energy
Manipulator and a Meta-morph with Energy
Manipulation capability is that an Energy Manipulator
does not change their physical, molecular state to either
generate or transfer energy (see META-MORPH).

FLIGHT:
Flight is the ability to fly, glide or levitate above the
Earth's surface without use of an external source (e.g.
jetpack). Flight can be accomplished through a variety of
methods, these include, but are not limited to:

- Reversing the forces of gravity
- Riding air currents
- Using planetary magnetic fields
- Wings

Metas exhibiting Flight can range from barely sustaining flight a few feet off the ground to reaching the far limits of outer space.

Often, Metas with Flight ability also display the complimentary ability of Super-Speed. However, it can be difficult to decipher if Super-Speed is a Meta power in its own right, or is simply a function of combining the Meta's Flight ability with the Earth's natural gravitational force.

MAGIC:

Magic is the ability to display a wide variety of Meta abilities by channeling the powers of a secondary magical or mystical source. Known secondary sources of Magic powers include, but are not limited to:

- Alien lifeforms
- Dark arts
- Demonic forces
- Departed souls
- Mystical spirits

Typically, the forces of Magic are channeled through an enchanted object. Known magical, enchanted objects include:

- Amulets
- Books
- Cloaks
- Gemstones
- Wands

- Weapons

Some Magicians have the ability to transport themselves into the mystical realm of their magical source. They may also have the ability to transport others into and out of these realms as well.

Note: the fundamental difference between a Magician and an Energy Manipulator is that a Magician typically channels their powers from a mystical source that likely requires use of an enchanted object to express these powers (see ENERGY MANIPULATOR).

META MANIPULATION:

Meta Manipulation is the ability to duplicate or negate the Meta powers of others. Meta Manipulation is a rare Meta power and can be extremely dangerous if the Meta Manipulator is capable of manipulating the powers of multiple Metas at one time. Meta Manipulators who can manipulate the powers of several Metas at once have been observed to reach Meta 4 power levels.

Based on the unique powers of the Meta Manipulator, it is hypothesized that other abilities could include altering or controlling the powers of others. Despite their tremendous abilities, Meta Manipulators are often unable to generate powers of their own, and are limited to manipulating the powers of others. When not utilizing their abilities, Meta Manipulators may be vulnerable to attack.

Note: It has been observed that a Meta Manipulator requires close physical proximity to a Meta target to fully manipulate their power. When fighting a Meta

Manipulator, it is advised to stay at a reasonable distance and to attack from long range. Meta Manipulators have been observed manipulating the powers of others up to 100 yards away.

META-MORPH:

Meta-morph is the ability to display a wide variety of Meta abilities by "morphing" all, or part, of one's physical form from one state into another. There are two sub-types of Meta-morphs:

- Physical
- Molecular

Physical morphing occurs when a Meta-morph transforms their physical state to express their powers. Physical Meta-morphs typically maintain their human physiology while exhibiting their powers (with the exception of Shape Shifters). Types of Physical morphing include, but are not limited to:

- Invisibility
- Malleability (elasticity/plasticity)
- Physical by-products (silk, toxins, etc…)
- Shape-shifting
- Size changes (larger or smaller)

Molecular morphing occurs when a Meta-morph transforms their molecular state from a normal physical state to a non-physical state to express their powers. Types of Molecular morphing include, but are not limited to:

- Fire
- Ice
- Rock
- Sand
- Steel
- Water

Note: Because Meta-morphs can display abilities that mimic all other Meta power classifications, it can be difficult to properly identify a Meta-morph upon first encounter. However, it is critical to carefully observe how their powers manifest, and, if it is through Physical or Molecular morphing, you can be certain you are dealing with a Meta-morph.

PSYCHIC:

Psychic is the ability to use one's mind as a weapon. There are two sub-types of Psychics:

- Telepaths
- Telekinetics

Telepathy is the ability to read and influence the thoughts of others. While Telepaths often do not appear to be physically intimidating, their power to penetrate minds can often result in more devastating damage than a physical assault.

Telekinesis is the ability to manipulate physical objects with one's mind. Telekinetics can often move objects with their mind that are much heavier than they could move physically. Many Telekinetics can also make objects move at very high speeds.

Note: Psychics are known to strike from long distance, and, in a fight it is advised to incapacitate them as quickly as possible. Psychics often become physically drained from extended use of their powers.

SUPER-INTELLIGENCE:
Super-Intelligence is the ability to display levels of intelligence above standard genius intellect. Super-Intelligence can manifest in many forms, including, but not limited to:

- Superior analytical ability
- Superior information synthesizing
- Superior learning capacity
- Superior reasoning skills

Note: Super-Intellects continuously push the envelope in the fields of technology, engineering, and weapons development. Super-Intellects are known to invent new approaches to accomplish previously impossible tasks. When dealing with a Super-Intellect, you should be mentally prepared to face challenges that have never been encountered before. In addition, Super-Intellects can come in all shapes and sizes. The most advanced Super-Intellects have originated from non-human creatures.

SUPER-SPEED:
Super-Speed is the ability to display movement at remarkable physical speeds above standard levels of speed. Metas with Super-Speed often exhibit complimentary abilities to movement that include, but are not limited to:

- Enhanced endurance
- Phasing through solid objects
- Super-fast reflexes
- Time travel

Note: Metas with super-speed often have an equally super metabolism, burning thousands of calories per minute, and requiring them to eat many extra meals a day to maintain consistent energy levels. It has been observed that Metas exhibiting Super-Speed are quick thinkers, making it difficult to keep up with their thought process.

SUPER-STRENGTH:

Super-Strength is the ability to utilize muscles to display remarkable levels of physical strength above expected levels of strength. Metas with Super-Strength are able to lift or push objects that are well beyond the capability of an average member of their species. Metas exhibiting Super-Strength can range from lifting objects twice their weight to incalculable levels of strength allowing for the movement of planets.

Metas with Super-Speed often exhibit complimentary abilities to strength that include, but are not limited to:

- Earthquake generation through stomping
- Enhanced jumping
- Invulnerability
- Shockwave generation through clapping

Note: Metas with Super-Strength may not always possess this strength evenly. Metas with Super-Strength have been observed to demonstrate powers in only one arm or leg.

META PROFILE CHARACTERISTICS

FROM THE META MONITOR:
In addition to having a strong working knowledge of a Meta's powers and capabilities, it is also imperative to have an understanding of the key characteristics that form the core of their character. When facing or teaming up with Metas, understanding their key characteristics will help you gain deeper insight into their mentality and strategic potential.

What follows is a brief explanation of the five key characteristics you should become familiar with. **Note:** the data that appears in each Meta profile has been compiled from live field activity.

COMBAT:
The ability to defeat a foe in hand-to-hand combat.

DURABILITY:
The ability to withstand significant wear, pressure or damage.

LEADERSHIP:
The ability to lead a team of disparate personalities and powers to victory.

STRATEGY:
The ability to find, and successfully exploit, a foe's weakness.

WILLPOWER:
The ability to persevere, despite seemingly insurmountable odds.

DON'T MISS EPIC ZERO 3

Elliott Harkness has learned the ropes and even saved the world a few times. But when he makes a major mistake during a do-or-die mission, his confidence is shattered and he decides to hang up his tights … for good.

Unfortunately, a new threat emerges that forces Elliott to put his early retirement plans on hold. A fiery cosmic creep known as the Herald is heading for Earth, and bringing Ravager—the Annihilator of Worlds—with him! With the end of everything quickly approaching, can Elliott become the epic hero he's destined to be? Or, will he always be just an Epic Zero?

Don't miss Epic Zero 3: Tales of a Super Lame Last Hope!

ACKNOWLEDGMENTS

Writers are notorious for spending much of their time alone—plotting, writing, and rewriting. While I certainly spent plenty of time alone, I never once felt alone, thanks to my amazing family. Thanks to Lynn—my partner, editor, and story consultant extraordinaire. Thanks to Olivia—my fountain of encouragement. And finally, thanks to Matthew—my daily creative inspiration.

ABOUT THE AUTHOR

By day, R.L. Ullman functions as a mild-mannered member of society. By night, he is an award-winning author who writes a never-ending battle for truth, justice and whatever he's feeling at the moment. He is a life-long fan of all things superhero and lives with his wife, kids and possibly evil cockapoo in Connecticut.

If you enjoyed Epic Zero 2, please leave a review to help others discover this series. By writing an honest review, you provide the necessary fuel to help Epic Zero 2 rocket up the rankings and get discovered by more readers just like you! Thanks for your support!

For news, updates, and exclusive content, please sign up for the Epic Newsflash at rlullman.com.